Emma Muir

God's Octave

And other Poems

Emma Muir

God's Octave
And other Poems

ISBN/EAN: 9783337401337

Printed in Europe, USA, Canada, Australia, Japan

Cover: Foto ©Andreas Hilbeck / pixelio.de

More available books at **www.hansebooks.com**

GOD'S OCTAVE

And Other Poems

BY

EMMA MUIR.

PRINTED FOR PRIVATE CIRCULATION.

TO THE READER.

THE following lines, which I feel are full of faults, I dedicate to my dear Husband.

Most of them have been written under the pressure of severe bodily and mental suffering; but if, through the power of God's grace, they are permitted to be the means by which some souls are led to a stronger faith, more earnest seeking, and truer child-like trust in God's love, what a cause for thankfulness there will be

To one so unworthy as,

Yours in Truth,

EMMA · MUIR.

123 HAM PARK ROAD,
WEST HAM, ESSEX,
March 21st, 1896.

CONTENTS.

GOD'S OCTAVE.

NIAGARA'S waters soundeth, on, on
    through night and day,
Under the silver moonbeams and sun-
    light's golden ray,
Those wondrous gathered waters, those
    remnants of the flood,
Their hymn ascendeth ever, unto the
    throne of God.

The dusky savage knew them in his
    wild hunting ground,
And there he gazed in wonder 'mid
    solitude profound ;
And *we* would gaze and worship where
    the dark savage stood,
Till our lips cried out in gladness, "Thy
    works, O God, are good."

9

For as our eyes were ravished by shades
of glowing light,
We'd revel in the beauty of mercy blent
with might,
That misty veil would show us the
octave of God's love,
Let down from " The Eternal," to lift
our hearts above.

Crimson, orange, yellow, green, blue,
dark indigo,
Majestically doth purple add to the
regal show,
Reflected in its vapour those rainbow
tints appear,
And to complete the octave, God's
white light shineth clear.

And is there not an octave in grace as
well as light,
Those spirit gifts Christ bought us, on
Calvary's dark night,
That crimson tide which, gushing forth
from His wounded side,

Gives us the power to love, God's love,
 through Him the Crucified.

Then faith shall bring contentment,
 while peace and hope will be
All ready with their garlands to crown
 humility ;
Till praise shall sound triumphant, our
 hearts with rapture beat,
Rejoicing that the octave of God's love
 is complete.

Just love in the beginning, from which
 this world hath grown,
And love, still love attending, around
 the great white throne,
And love shall tune the voices, the keynote " Love " will be,
Of never-ending sweetness, all through
 eternity.

BUT BY ME.

Seven letters, did they stand
As the motto of our land,
Blazoned forth in gold and gem
Richer than queen's diadem,
That the people all might see,
No man cometh, "But by Me."

Seven letters, carve them deep
Into oaken bas-relief,
On the pulpit, arras, stall,
Where they may be read by all—
Rich and poor alike may see,
No man cometh, "But by Me."

Seven letters, let them trace
Filigree as fine as lace;
Costly ornaments to vie
With the gifts the rich ones buy;
Then those wealthy ones might see,
No man cometh, "But by Me."

Seven letters, pure and white,
Cut in polished marble bright ;
Place them on the holy dead
Waiting Christ their living Head,
That their followers might see,
No man cometh, " But by Me."

Seven letters, write in gold,
Quaint device as missal old ;
Bind in skin or velvet rare,
Fitted for some lady fair,
That the dainty one might see,
No man cometh, " But by Me."

Seven letters, let them print
In the black or coloured ink ;
Hang them near the thronging crowd
Where the engine whistles loud,
So the busy one may see,
No man cometh, " But by Me."

Seven letters, large and clear,
On the mission wall appear,

Then those sad ones, sick of sin,
May a gleam of comfort win;
Till by faith they too may see,
No man cometh, " But by Me."

Seven letters, let them rule
In the day and Sabbath school,
Shine with love into the heart,
Winning each to do their part;
Young bright eyes would quickly see,
No man cometh, " But by Me."

Seven letters, oh! how grand,
As we learn to understand,
Surely shall our hearts rejoice
" That one way " is God's own choice.
Grant us, Lord, Thy grace to be
Daily nearer God, by Thee.

GOD'S WILL.

My God, if I could only know
 The sweet completeness of Thy will,
Then should my heart with rapture glow,
 And every pulse with joy would thrill.

Thy will! which gathered all the light
   Out from the darkness, drew the line
Which separates the day from night,
   Giving to us the thought of time.

Thy will! which formed the spider's web
   To hold the mist of autumn morn,
Till brilliant sunbeams light each thread
   And it to jewel-case transform.

Thy will! which caused the thunder crash,
   And sent the lightning's vivid gleam,
Made minnow's tiny fin to splash
   The water of the rippling stream.

Thy will! by which the Alps uprose,
   Showing the sunrise light sublime,
Gave to the valley sweet repose,
   Where glow-worm's tiny lamp doth
     shine.

Thy will held ocean's expanse vast,
   Each tiny seed and wayside flower,
The meteor as it glances past,
   And every drop of summer shower.

Thy will! which gave each bonnie bird
    The plan and skill its nest to build,
And then with love their bosom stirred
    To tend the nest when it is filled.

The form of leaf on plant or tree,
    The smallest insect flitting by,
The wondrous working of the bee,
    And feathered down on butterfly.

Thy will decreed and man was made,
    A breathing, thinking, living soul ;
Put into Eden's flowery glade,
    And heaven for his destined goal.

Thy will sent prophets, priests, and kings
    To teach that will until the time
Was ready for the purer things,
    Which showed how Love and Will
    combine.

Thy will a fitted body framed,
    In which Thy only Son could dwell ;
Through it the Godhead was proclaimed
    By Jesus, our Emmanuel.

Thy will He came and lived to do,
  Perfect each step the way He trod,
Grand in obedience, nobly true,
  Living near Him our soul finds God.

NOT I, BUT CHRIST WHO DWELLETH IN ME.

NOT I, not I,
For this is worthless trash ;
  Not I, not I,
Impetuous, weak, and rash ;
  Not I, not I,
Frail as a rope of sand,
  Not I, not I,
But He who can command
  This worthless I,
And work in me His will,
  Until I hear
His blessed " Peace, be still,"
  Drink in His love,
And find my work and rest,
  Lost unto self,
Upon " The Master's breast."

B

LET DOWN THE NETS.

O SIMON, Simon, oft do we
Just take our pattern straight from thee,
    And letting down one net
Think we have really done
    The Master's will, while we forget
    He has some gracious purpose yet,
Some blessing to be won ;
    And so we lose the larger share,
    For want of a more thoughtful care.

The nets were needed safe to keep
That draught of fishes from the deep,
    Which waited but His word,
In thronging numbers press
    His will to do whose voice they heard ;
    Their action never was deferred,
And why should we do less ?
    To us how much of joy is lost,
    What does our slack obedience cost ?

The finny tribe a lesson teach,
Though wisdom was beyond their reach

They hear but to obey,
And broken nets can tell
   The wondrous blessing will not stay,
   But come in His appointed way
Who doeth all things well ;
   Oh, for the listening ear and heart !
   That we may humbly do our part.

And conscience bids us oft beware,
That many nets we need in prayer ;
   And, did we use them right,
Would not all grumbles flee,
   And faith grow stronger far than
     sight,
   While brain and heart and hand unite
To work right steadily ;
   If all our nets were held quite still,
   How quickly would the Master fill !

Our waiting net must ready be,
For blessings oft come speedily ;
   At other times they wait
Till He sees fit to send
   His royal messenger of state

Round by the way of patience gate
Unto the wished-for end.
   Oh! may we not lose one delight
   Through any hasty walk by sight.

Our net of faith must strengthened be
At every opportunity,
   Or prayer will soon grow cold ;
But if each knot be true,
No circumstance will break it through,
   And we to Christ shall firmly hold ;
Good work in us He'll do,
   And will our swift obedience see
   Letting both nets down to the sea.

TRUE LIFE.

OH! for the Life, the free, free Life,
   That Life which God can give,
The 'bounding joy, without alloy,
   When Christ in us doth live.

This Life hath peace, the sweet, sweet
    Inward heavenly balm ;   [peace,
Showing our sin hath full release,
    Keeping the heart so calm.

And with this peace hope ever dwells,
    Sending its cheering ray
Through every adverse circumstance
    We meet with, day by day.

Then love, real love, deep, earnest, true,
    Which like a golden band
Surrounds us every passing hour,
    Placed by Almighty hand.

We hold it all, by mystic power,
    Faith in the Living Word ;
Through it the wonderful Unseen
    Is known, and felt, and heard.

O Lord, we ask this gift of Thine,
    That daily we may be
Filled with an impulse all Divine
    Of Immortality.

For life holds no monotony
  Where spirit-power leads,
Each day is filled by circles new
  Of loving words and deeds.

The brain so charged with thought and
  Yet holds no anxious care ;   [plan,
Nothing then frets the inward man,
  No trial brings despair.

We know Thy will is one with ours,
  Fully to sanctify,
So wait the Pentecostal gift,
  Thy Spirit drawing nigh.

———

ALL THINGS.

"And we know that all things work together for good to those who love God."—ROMANS viii. 28.

How mighty the Love,
  Which the Father above,
Has promised to give to His child ;
  It will conquer the sin,

And all evil within,
As we grow in His grace meek and mild.

Omnipotent charm,
That defends from all harm
Each one who will trust to its power;
And waiting His will,
Find the promise fulfil,
Working good towards us every hour.

Do *we* love the Lord,
Then *no* thing should afford
Us a sorrow, a worry, or care;
Each case *He* will meet,
For His work is complete,
Giving strength every burden to bear.

Should dark clouds appear,
Still there's *no* thing to fear—
They will strengthen our faith while they
The more we submit,   [stay;
Then the more we are fit
To give thanks when those clouds pass
away.

Oh, can we but say
That we grow every day
In true love to God, Father, and Son
Then all will be right,
Until faith becomes sight,
For on earth this is heaven begun.

A PRAYER.

I PLEAD Thy Name, O Jesus,
　For I am full of sin ;
Washed in Thy blood most precious,
　I shall be pure within.

My faith is very feeble,
　My doubts like mountains rise,
I cannot grasp a promise
　To check these tears and sighs.

I plead Thy name, O Jesus,
　Soften this heart of stone ;
Pour in the Balm of Gilead
　To make it all Thine own.

Thine, thine must be the work, Lord!
   Mine be the sin and shame;
That I no more have sought Thee,
   No more believed Thy Name.

Oh, draw me to Thyself, now,
   By love's own silken band;
Then gentleness and patience
   Shall be at my command.

May meekness, modest flower,
   Within my heart abide,
And sweet smooth-browed contentment
   Be ever at my side.

Then Peace's pure snowy petals
   Thy Love, Lord, shall reveal,
And joy's bright ruby tints show
   Thy gracious power to heal.

May every Christ-like grace, Lord,
   Find resting-place in me,
And from all sin and self, Lord,
   For ever set me free.

Oh, by Thy Spirit's power,
  Grant this my earnest prayer;
Then from that very hour
  I shall lose every care.

Then shall my faith be firm, Lord,
  Then shall I walk Thy ways,
And with Thy saints on earth, Lord,
  Sing my Redeemer's praise.

NO SEPARATION.

ROMANS viii. 37.

No thing can separate the soul
  Which daily grows in Love,
Seeking its strength and nourishment
  From Him who dwells above.

Each trial then becomes a means
  Of gain and not of loss,
Because we cheerfully take it up,
  And bear it near His Cross.

So no distress can ever hurt
　Us, if we trust in Him,
For *He* has paid the wondrous price
　To ransom us from sin.

For Love He would not save Himself
　One pang, that we might be
Just living monuments of grace,
　From doubt and darkness free.

Feeling each day we grow more near
　Unto His wounded side ;
For in His love we find our strength,
　Whatever may betide.

No separation from our God,
　Who makes this world so bright,
That even here He satisfies
　And gives us true delight.

It is the spring of all our joys,
　The life of our desire,
A growing, living power within,
　A baptism of fire.

Grant, Lord, that we may really know
  The sweetness of this thought,
For then shall we begin in truth
  To serve Thee as we ought.

EXAMPLE.

Oh, strangely wonderful, mysteriously
  strange,
That power we are compelled to use
  throughout our life;
No matter where or how we live, we
  cannot free ourselves
From that strange force, which aids in
  peace or strife.

We do not trace one wave of thought
  unto its root,
Nor follow all the windings, subtle, deep,
  and keen;
Oft do not note their power until we
  find the fruit,

And then we sigh and say, Alas! what
    might have been.

That influence which quite unconsciously
    we use,
May be but one swift glance, born of a
    passing thought,
Touches that other life, and leaves its
    impress there,
To aid in weal or woe the change that
    glance hath wrought.

Responsibilities encircling every life,
As spirit's gaze grows clear, thy vastness
    on us loom,
And we begin to trace though but the
    outer edge
Of God's great plan of Love ; no fearful
    fiery doom,

But everlasting love, that promises to
    all
The strength, in full supply, to learn to
    live to grow

Into the image of His Son Divine, our
   Lord,
That we may know the Love from
   which our love must flow.

More strangely wonderful, mysteri-
   ously strange
Becomes the daily life when lifted into
   Christ ;
Our thoughts, looks, words, and wishes,
   never from Him range,
We have no anxious care, quite sure we
   are led right.

Touching infinitude, the dignity of life
   steps in,
And day by day, yes, hour by hour, we
   see
E'en in the busy toil, the rush of life is
   rife
With power unseen but felt, linked to
   eternity.

Oh, God, as Thou wouldst have our lives
   to be like Thine,

Lift us, each day, more near Thine
  unseen Love,
Till we become an echo of Thy truth
  sublime,
And find this world as full of Thee, as
  heaven above.

Then recognise each one we meet as
  being Thine,
Therefore our help to them must spring
  direct from Thee ;
Let it but bear Thy touch, it shall
  entwine
Some thought, look, word, or act, in true
  purity.

Father, we now would give our all into
  Thy care,
Work Thou Thy will in us, till we clear
  caskets are
To hold Thy glory, and then by love be
  made to share
Thyself; so we as scintillating light shall
  shine afar.

I NEED THEE EVERY HOUR.

I NEED Thee every hour,
　My heart cries out for Thee ;
I want by faith to know Thee,
　And Thy great love for me.

I need Thee every hour,
　On, on through all my life ;
That Thy own strength may aid me
　In all my daily strife.

I need Thee every hour,
　I cannot stand alone ;
My enemies are mighty,
　Their strength 's beyond my own.

I need Thee every hour,
　I know not what will come ;
When Satan next will tempt me,
　What *work* should *next* be done.

I need Thee every hour,
   Lest I a chance should lose
Of growing in Thy likeness,
   And working as Thou choose.

I need Thee every hour,
   For thought and mind and heart
Must have its constant portion,
   To be of *Thee* a part.

I need Thee every hour,
   For sin wears strange disguise;
Dark looks light to finite sight,
   And daze my mental eyes.

I need Thee every hour
   In all my work or rest;
Lest ease too much should tempt me,
   And *work* fail to be best.

I need Thee every hour,
   That others, too, may see
How sweet and bright may be a life,
   When *all* is spent with Thee.

c

And, oh, my heart throbs quickly,
　　The tears bedew mine eyes,
To think my supplication
　　Is heard beyond the skies.

And soon will come the answer :
　　My child, I'm close to thee,
And faith shall make it clearer
　　Till thou My face shall see.

I WILL.

"I *will* keep him in perfect peace, whose mind is
stayed on Me, because he trusteth in Me."

How wonderful the promise,
　　Which towers thus on high !
Like grand and mighty mountain peaks
　　Clear cut against the sky ;
It stands so sure and steadfast,
　　A help in every ill,
Shall we not rest upon the strength
　　Of God's complete—I will ?

'Tis spoken by the Father,
   Therefore we *must* believe,
For He is our unchanging God,
   And never will deceive ;
So, every doubt must vanish,
   All murmuring be still ;
Ah, let it sink into our hearts,
   His glorious—I will.

And closely linked unto it,
   There soundeth full and free,
The separate call that makes it
   So fit for you and me ;
Fresh as a sparkling fountain
   Which bubbles to the brim,
Enough for each, the love of God,
   Which says—I will keep him.

Yet fuller grows the promise ;
   God condescends to show
The way in which He keepeth those
   Who in His grace doth grow.
How true and free and perfect
   Is that divine release !

God, Father, Son, and Spirit,
 Will keep in—Perfect Peace.

And now, like sunset glory,
 It bursts upon the view,
Showing the tender depth and power
 Of God's love, pure and true.
No hard command He gives us,
 But sayeth constantly—
I will keep him in perfect peace,
 Because he trusteth *Me.*

Oh, how we yearn to have it,
 That peace which God can give!
Oh, how we pant to know it,
 That peace in Christ to live!
And yet, how clear and simple,
 A child the truth might see,
I will keep him in perfect peace,
 Whose mind is stayed on Thee.

TRIALS NOT TROUBLES.

To M. P.

NEARER to Him,
Then can they troubled be?
Nearer to that
Which doth enlighten me;
Nearer to Him
Who all the work hath done,
Nearer to that
Which shows the victory won.
Nearer to Him
Who gives the glad release;
Nearer to that
Which brings my spirit's peace.
Nearer to Him
Who bore the cross and shame;
Nearer to that
Which makes us love His name.
Nearer to Him
Whom it is joy to know;
Nearer to that
Which healeth all my woe.

Quite near to Him,
Then life indeed is bliss ;
       And all things must be good,
Which lead to this.

———

UNSELFISHNESS.

Written for E. R.

OH, virtue pure, that bears the sway,
We'd crown thee aye with royal bay,
And bid thee with us ever stay,
              Unselfishness.

The dullest spot thou canst make bright,
And homely tasks with power incite ;
Till hearts shall beat with true delight,
              Unselfishness.

In many a home how sweet thou art,
So noiselessly thou dost thy part,
Quietly healing wounds that smart,
              Unselfishness.

No pettishness can dwell with thee,
From sullen looks thou art quite free,
And hidden blessings thou canst see,
                Unselfishness.

In thee real patience has her work,
No trying duty wilt thou shirk,
And no one's feelings canst thou hurt,
                Unselfishness.

Numberless burdens thou wilt bear,
Making another's good thy care ;
Willing thy joy with them to share,
                Unselfishness.

What pure enjoyment thou dost bring !
Coming like bird on silent wing,
Sweet as the balmy breath of spring,
                Unselfishness.

Yet oft unnoticed dost thou dwell
'Midst selfish ones, who cannot tell
From whence the power that serves them
    well,   Unselfishness.

When we begin to know thy worth,
And that great Love that gave thee birth
And scatters thee o'er all the earth,
                    Unselfishness ;

Then, then we want thy way to learn,
Clearly thy beauty to discern ;
And pray our hearts may hold thy germ,
                    Unselfishness.

—————

MIDNIGHT THOUGHTS.

In the silence of the midnight
    Do the spirits hold control,
And whisper solemn secrets
    To the humble waiting soul.

In the silence of the midnight
    How I long Thy love to know,
Falling like a benediction,
    Healing all my sin and woe.

In the silence of the midnight
  I would lift my heart to Thee,
And beseech a revelation
  Of the sweetest mystery.

In the silence of the midnight
  I the spirit's touch would feel,
To make Thy cross and sacrifice
  So near, so true, and real.

In the silence of the midnight
  Then a living Lord I need,
With tender love and sympathy
  To give me strength indeed.

In the silence of the midnight
  To this hope my spirit clings,
And o'er me it seems hovering
  Like the waft of angel wings.

In the silence of the midnight
  I need more than words express;
A loving, growing consciousness
  Of Thy sweet peace and rest.

JESUS ONLY.

St. Mark ix. 8.

Jesus only, Jesus only,
  'Tis Thy face we wish to see;
When we are most sad and lonely
  We would find our rest in Thee.

Jesus only, help us onward
  Through the trouble of each day;
Though with stumbling steps and slow,
    Lord,
  Keep us in the narrow way.

Jesus only, when in danger
  Unto Thee for help we call;
Thou whose bed was lowly manger
  Now hast power over all.

Jesus only, let Thy presence
  Take possession of our heart;
May we feel Thy very essence,
  Then from Thee we ne'er can part.

'Tis the same, the old, old story,
　　Unto Thee our voice we raise ;
When in heaven's perfect glory,
　　Jesus only ! still our praise.

REAL LOVE.

ONE angry word or one cold look,
　　How deep the pain 'twill bring !
Acting as frost upon a brook,
　　To check its gushing spring.

As the full current deep and strong
　　Leaps o'er its pebbly bed,
So flows the tide of love along
　　By looks, words, actions fed.

But if the streamlet shallow be,
　　No bright green turf be near,
If shaded by no spreading tree,
　　It soon will disappear.

The weary traveller in vain
　　May seek his thirst to quell,
No sparkling drops or verdant plain
　　Of murmuring waters tell.

And so if love be weak and poor,
　　'Twill surely pass away;
For tiny trifles, light as air,
　　Will wear it day by day.

But if the love be firm and pure—
　　True, constant, brave and strong—
Each trial will make it more secure,
　　And bear it safely on.

If, at the very spring of love,
　　Real trust stands strong and brave,
Guarding it like a spreading tree,
　　Affords a leafy shade,

Then confidence and candour sweet
　　Will e'en go hand in hand ;
Truth, gentleness, and patience meet
　　To form a noble band.

If, as deep banks of verdant green,
  Religion's pleasant ways
Guard either side of love's pure stream
  From sin and Satan's rage,

Then fear ye not that love is true,
  It ever will abide ;
No time or trial, friend or foe,
  Can check its flowing tide.

But where can such a love be found,
  Such height of human bliss ?
Beats there a heart in all around
  That feels a love like this?

Oh, doubt it not, but own the sway
  Of love's most mighty powers ;
And then in truth we 'll humbly say,
  Yes ! such a love is ours.

———

FREEDOM IN CHRIST.

ROMANS viii. 2.

THY spirit's law hath made me free,
Oh, glorious thought is this to me,
I know I owe it all to Thee,
　　My Lord and God.

No claim is there in aught I do,
The grace and power comes all from you,
And my right actions, oh, how few !
　　Jesus my King.

What should I be without Thy grace,
Bereft of faith, to see Thy face,
How woful then would be my case,
　　Redeemer Christ.

Help me to feel it more each day,
In everything I do or say;
May it be Thine, not mine the way,
　　Jehovah Lord.

Let self be daily crucified,
And I live nearer to Thy side ;
That Thou, not I, be deified,
　O King of kings !

NOTHING TO FEAR.

ROMANS viii. 31.

NOTHING to fear, my soul, nothing to
　fear !
In every time of doubt, Jesus is near ;
By His omnipotence, mighty to save,
Through the great ransom paid, *death* is
　His slave ;
Only by faith look up, all will be clear,
Rest in His love complete, nothing to
　fear.

Satan comes creeping near, tempting to
　sin,
Hard thoughts and discontent murmur
　within ;

Self then will try to rule, strive for the
    prize,
Friends often prove but foes, though in
    disguise ;
When everything in life looks so severe,
Still amid all this strife, nothing to fear.

What spear can pierce the shield faith
    gives to thee ?
Girt with God's truth around, art thou
    not free ?
Shod with the peace He gives, safe
    canst thou tread,
Salvation's helmet to cover thine head,
E'en through the starless night, though
    dark and drear,
Lift up thy voice and cry, Nothing to fear.

Stand by the pebbly beach, where is the
    bound,
Yon mighty wave will dash with solemn
    sound,
Tearing with giant strength, rock, cliff
    and strand,

Wreathing with scattered foam each
    point of land ;
But see that tiny child, precious and
    dear,
Plays *past* the water-mark, nothing to
    fear.

In those dim ages back long, long ago,
God spake that "hitherto" each wave
    should know ;
So every foe thou hast cannot step o'er,
For, like that "hitherto" guarding the
    shore,
God fights upon your side, safe will He
    steer,
You can in triumph cry, Nothing to fear.

YE ASK AND HAVE NOT.

To Mrs. P.

Is it so, Lord, have I been asking Thee
In some wrong way, for what I yearn to
    see ?

D

Is it so, Lord, a something in the way
I thee have sought, and still most earnest
    pray?

Or is it, Lord, some doubt that takes
        away   [day?
The resting trust, as I seek Thee each

Or is it, Lord, that Satan takes this
    Word,
And makes me doubt my prayer will
    find Thee, Lord?

Full well he knows where best to find
    his dart,
And from Thy Word, can pierce into my
    heart.

So artful he a form like angel's make,
And my dazed sight may of his wrong
    partake;

And he would keep me with a despot's
        rod,   [his God.
Who took the Word and dared to tempt

Lord Jesus, now lift up the veil that lies
Between Thy love and my poor mental
    eyes,

That I may see Thee as indeed Thou
    art,
Then not a doubt shall touch my faith-
    filled heart.

LET.

"Let him take hold of My strength that he may
make peace with Me, and he *shall* make peace with
Me."—ISAIAH xxvii. 5.

LORD, this *Let* seems to me like a grand,
    mighty mountain,
  Too high and too noble for my strength
    to climb ;
So I turn unto Thee for a draught from
    Thy fountain,
  To aid me drink in this permission
    sublime.

Let, and may tell me much that my
    heart now doth covet,
  To know Thou art willing Thy
    strength to impart,
To accept each command finding soul
    and mind, love it—
  Ah, this is Thy strength, Lord, I need
    in my heart.

Strength to grasp the full grace which
    Thy love now doth proffer,
  And find Thy peace glowing through
    heart, mind, and soul,
Not in fear turn away from Thy wonder-
    ful offer,
  But give *all self* up to Thy loving
    control.

For hast not Thou set, in Thy great
    condescension,
  Thy seal with its " shall thus " to cast
    out each fear,

No, not hell, with its prince, dare curtail
    the dimension,
    Of love, light, and strength, which that
    "shall" bringeth near.

Wrapped up in a peace which trans-
    cendeth the telling,
    For words are too weak the full force
    to impart,
It only is known by the Spirit's indwell-
    ing,
    Revealing God's love to the sanctified
    heart.

THY STRENGTH IS AS THY DAY.

As very weak and weary,
    In quietness I lay,
These words came sweet and clearly—
    Thy strength is as thy day.

No need just now for power,
  My work is to lie still
And patiently be learning,
  Then bow unto Thy will.

Thou knowest I am feeble,
  My strength is very small ;
The Cross Thou givest to me
  Is hard indeed for all.

Help me to trust Thy wisdom,
  And rest me in Thy love ;
To hear Thy voice sound softly
  To me from heaven above.

Thy spirit's eye shall open
  To see the work is Mine,
The Holy Ghost shall lead thee
  To knowledge more Divine.

Each lesson shall grow sweeter,
  Each joy more purely glow ;
The fount of living waters,
  Thy thirsty soul o'erflow.

Thou wilt look up in gladness,
　Though weak may be thy frame;
Each sign of gloom and sadness
　Will flee before My name.

Believe I am thy Saviour,
　Thy ransom I have paid,
A crown of endless glory
　For thee in heaven laid.

Is thy name surely written
　In the Lamb's Book of Life?
Then, where should be thy trouble,
　Thy doubts, and fears, or strife?

Canst thou not rest thee calmly
　Within My arms of love,
And feel that I will bear thee
　Safe to the home above?

And then the sweet sound faded,
　While brighter grew the dawn;
The light o'er moor and mountain
　Proclaim another morn.

A calm content came o'er me,
  I felt God's ways are best ;
I 'll humbly strive to trust Him,
  And leave to Him the rest.

— — —

AM I HIS CHILD?

ROMANS viii. 17.

OH, mighty If, how great Thou art !
  Where doth Thou stand for me ?
A portal to the highest bliss,
  On God's good just decree.

Can I say, Yes, I am His child,
  What wondrous view folds out !
For time, and for eternity,
  Without one fear or doubt.

For if a child, why, then an heir—
  The thought's almost *too* grand ;
If 'twas not from the Lord Himself,
  We could not understand.

An heir of *God*, what's hid beneath
  Those words of truth sublime?
Why, *ever* growing holiness,
  Through *all* my span of time.

For as the heir when of right age
  Should *be* fit to inherit
Whatever wealth his father left,
  So *shall* we grow in spirit.

Our Father's hand will guide His child
  Safe through all toil and danger;
Daily more fit to share with Him,
  Whose cradle was a manger.

And as from dawn the growing light
  Brightens to noon-day splendour,
So all through life our hearts to Him
  A glowing love shall render.

Oh, joyful thought, a child of God,
  An heir of heaven's brightness;
How beautiful each life will be
  Stamped with the Saviour's likeness.

WHAT CAN YOU DO?

Written for a School Recitation.

A FIERCE battle is raging around us each
    day,
Of what wondrous powers no mortal
    can say;
It appeals, fellow-creature, to me and to
    you,
With the heart searching question,
            Now, what can you do?

In this battle I speak of, no steel may
    appear,
No visible armour, or glittering spear;
But it cries to us all, Will you fight with
    the few?
Oh, answer this question!
            Say, what can you do?

There's no rich silken banner, or charger
    so bold,

No gorgeous procession our senses to
    hold ;
But it pleads with a might, There is
    right with the few,
Now, brother, pray tell us,
            Which part can you do ?

There's no time to be lost, if we'd help
    in the fray,
For our brothers and sisters are passing
    away ;
And if we have power to aid but the
    few,
Shall we waste it by failing
            In what we can do ?

The Generals are mighty which lead on
    the van,
With deep skill and knowledge their
    armies they plan ;
And the cry still goes on with its accent
    so true,
Come, sisters, and tell us,
            Which part can you do ?

Do you know the Great Captain, who
    leads the small band,
A strong faith can see Him, so noble He
    stands ;
He cheers up the faint-hearted with love
    strong and true,
And gives to the weakest,
                  Some part they can do.

Oh, believe there is power with those on
    the right,
See how firm, true, and steadfast, they
    stand in the fight ;
They know that the victory will come
    to the few,
And no doubt mars the action
                  In what they can do.

There patience is waiting for what may
    betide,
And content, her twin sister, stands
    close to her side ;
Faith, so clear-eyed and strong, with
    gaze full and true,

And hope, beaming with gladness, is
    following too ;
Kindness there is, all ready to place on
    the brow
Of thrift, temperance, and labour, the
    laurels won now ;
Humility 's willing to take a small place,
That trust, goodness, and meekness
    have their own in the race.   [band,
But time would me fail to tell how that
In this wondrous battle fight close hand
    to hand.

But gaze on that phalanx where many
    are seen,
What fearful companions are found
    there I ween.
If they held up their character full to
    our view,
We should cry out in horror,
              Oh ! what can I do?

There is self in all grades, from cobbler
    to king,

Deceit offering honey, under which is
    the sting;
There is envy's false smile, her feelings
    to hide,
Black hate, in rebellion all rule to
    deride;
Impudence ready his foes to attack,
And greed failing to fight through the
    load on his back.
There is luxury and sloth, anger, artful-
    ness, strife,
Despair's downward look—what's his
    interest in life?
Indifference comes slow, discontent very
    near,
Suspicion's quick start and sly stealthy
    leer;
Unitarian, deist, drunkard, and thief,
With some great men of Science;
But my list shall be brief,
For we shrink to take time with so fear-
    ful a crew,
Yet they show us each moment,
            There's much work to do.

But their leader is artful, so subtle and
    strong,
He looks well about him while marching
    along ;
And if some weak straggler's apart from
    the few,
He will send one to tempt him with
            Great things to do.

Though we all have our duties, yet oft
    in a day
There are moments of time we would
    well give away
To win from the many, and strengthen
    the few,
For there's always work waiting that
            Each one can do.

So look to our Captain, He is waiting
    quite near,
With strong loving power our small
    barks to steer,

He will show the best way we can add
    to the few,
Then we never need doubt as to
        What we can do.

———

POSSIBILITIES OF GRACE.

POSSIBILITIES of Grace,
Has my pen the power to trace
How we speed upon the race,
      Under the banner of Jesus!

Oh, the grace of faith how strong!
It will deepen as we go on
Doing right and shunning wrong,
      Under the banner of Jesus.

Grace of love, how sweet art thou!
Our glad hearts to thee will bow,
Brightly pressing on just now,
      Under the banner of Jesus.

Grace of peace, what wondrous power
Comes from thee when sorrows lour,
Calmness grows with every hour,
   Under the banner of Jesus.

Grace of patience, true and meek,
How thy growth we daily seek!
Knowing thou wilt aid the weak,
   Under the banner of Jesus.

Sweet content, how dost thou spread
Feast for those who truly fed
By thy power and onward led,
   Under the banner of Jesus.

Gratitude, how dost thou bring
Speedy blessings from our King!
Higher still our praise shall ring,
   Under the banner of Jesus.

Humility, O grace so rare,
Pure as lily wondrous fair;
Yet in thee we have full share,
   Under the banner of Jesus.

E

Joy, thou perfume of all grace,
Thou wilt gild our daily race,
Stamping on each hour thy trace,
   Under the banner of Jesus.

Holy Spirit now reveal
Christ unto us, till we feel
His indwelling power is real,
   And we live by faith in Jesus.

PRAY ON.

PRAY on, pray on, O troubled soul,
 Though darkness dense as night
Hath wrapt thee like a garment round,
 And thou canst see no light.

Pray on, pray on ; there 's peace and rest,
 And deep full joy to come,
Before you gain the Heavenly land,
 If God's will 's fully done.

Pray on, pray on, the light shines clear,
 Doubt not nor be dismayed ;

The power of perfect trust will come,
  Though for a time delayed.

Pray on, pray on, though words should
    fail,
  And helpless seem thy case ;
God only waits until we see
  The light from Jesus' face.

Pray on, pray on, still take thy need,
  That burning wish of thine,
Close to the Cross, look up and see
  The human and Divine.

Pray on, pray on, with earnest zeal,
  Give doubt no time to rest,
For that will but delay the peace
  You need within your breast.

Pray on, pray on, ask not the why,
  For that is not thy part ;
The why is with the great I Am,
  Who readeth every heart.

Pray on, pray till self-consciousness
  Is crucified in Him,
Then grace renews what sin hath made
  So foully stained and dim.

Pray on, pray till His image grows
  To likeness all can trace,
For living Him thou wilt become
  A monument of grace.

Pray on, pray on, *till* prayer becomes
  A lower note of praise,
Then peace and joy and work be thine
  With Him through all thy days.

———

IN THE NAME OF JESUS.

WHAT a gleam of brightness, doth His
  name bestow !   [below ;
Glinting on the actions of His saints
What a light of glory will His name
  afford !   [Lord.
In the heavenly mansions of our risen

Tiny cup of water, given in His
name,
Brings a richer blessing than some deeds
of fame;
In the light of heaven will the ran-
somed sing,
Joyfully receiving praises from their
King.

Words and deeds of kindness, done in
Jesus' name,
Though unknown to others, on Him
have a claim;
And in heaven's brightness, how each
deed will shine!
As it bears a likeness to our Lord
Divine.

Poor and all unworthy as each act may
seem—
Slight and unsubstantial, as phases of a
dream,

Yet look, word, and action, done for
    Christ the King,
Shine with a perfection nothing else
    will bring.

How they glow and glitter in the glori-
    ous light!
Where no sun is needed, where there is
    no night,
As the glory chaseth all the gloom
    away,
For Jesus is the brightness of that end-
    less day.

I ASK NOT THE WHY.

Why taken to London at all?
    That's a nut I defy you to crack,
It's too much for a mouth large or
    small;
    Though Satan suggests an attack.

Why taken to breathe in the air
   That was poison to every part,
Making pain so much harder to bear,
   And nerves so much quicker to start?

Why, why, should the money be lost,
   Pass away like a storm in the wind;
Or as boat in a tempest be tossed,
   Till it leaves not a vestige behind?

Why, why, should the artful ones thrive
   And flourish, like bay tree so green,
While the honest ones struggle and strive,
   Through deep waters and trials un-
     seen?

Why, why, should the pain often rack?
   Is a problem he'd fain have me try,
And follow the tortuous track,
   To find out that wonderful why.

Ah, Satan! but that is your case:
   You could give me fine reasons by
     dozens—

But in every one I could trace
    Such a likeness, that makes them
        first cousins.

You say, Find out the why, and there 'll be
    A clear light on the path you can
        tread,
All mystery be taken from thee,
    And knowledge be granted instead.

You say, Why is the key that unlocks
    The gate of that palace so fair ?
Once enter, no other thing blocks
    One way to the joys that are there.

Now, Satan, be off with your why !
    With *that* I have nothing to do ;
It's strength I'm not going to try,
    For 'tis held by one stronger than you.

He knows this mysterious why ;
    I'm content it should rest in the hand
That was pierced, soul and body to buy,
    With a love that we can't understand.

Love that promises nothing shall harm,
  But *all things* shall work for our
    good;
Love that keeps the soul restful and
    calm,
  To the body sends clothing and food ;

Love that gives the mind quiet and
    peace,
  Causing each anxious fear to depart,
Making all our best powers increase,
  Till Christ dwell by faith in our heart.

So, Satan, be off with your why !
  An answer I 've given to thee ;
No doubt, you will other souls try,
  But this time you 've quite failed with
    me.

TO MY HUSBAND.

FAIN would I greet the thirty-first
With deeper sense of all your worth ;
And tender wishes, warm and true,
That richest blessings rest on you.
Through the changes of the year,
May there be no doubt or fear ;
Every step be taken right,
Feeling all is in God's sight ;
Trust His wisdom and His grace,
To fix aright our dwelling-place,
To fix it where, through this life's day,
We best may tread the narrow way.
Finding joy with one another,
Giving help to friend or brother,
Have what's good for strength and
     health,
Better far than worldly wealth,
And peaceful Sabbaths as they come
Sanctifying all the home.

I feel as if I now could creep
Close to God's footstool and there keep,

To think that I 've no power to be
A better helpmeet unto thee.
So many things I long to do,
That would bring comfort unto you ;
For all your burdens I would share,
And give my help in every care—
Oft meet you with a glad surprise
To bring the brightness to your eyes ;
Lighten the shadows of the way
In cheerful spirits day by day.

But this has all been put aside—
God bids me quietly abide
And do the work He gives to me,
Instead of that I want for thee.
And so *His work must be the best ;*
In this great thought I fain would
    rest,
That by His grace I 'll help you most,
Rightly to seek the Holy Ghost ;
Help in the wondrous mental strife
Which must be in Spirit's life,
Must be in all who strive to tread
In the same steps where Jesus led.

Higher and higher onward still
Until we glory in God's will;
And if this grace be granted me,
Then a real helpmeet shall I be:
Content through all this care and pain,
Content to find my loss thy gain.
Content until in endless day
Our God shall wipe all tears away,
And you and I together be
Happy through all Eternity.

WALL-FLOWERS.

ONE of the first to show my buds
    Amid the clustering green;
One of the last to fade away
    Before the north wind keen.

I need no gardener's tender care
    To make me blossom right,
No house of glass or heated stove
    To bring forth petals bright.

A little cranny in the wall
  Holds room enough for me ;
If there my tiny seed should fall,
  I bloom both full and free.

Up, up, upon some lofty tower,
  My banner streams on high,
My yellow buds and bright green leaves
  Seen clear against the sky.

How fine I look in some bit spot
  Beside a cottage door ;
Of flowers striped and crimson dyed
  I show a goodly store.

The children as they go to school
  Will gather many a spray,
Inhale my perfume with delight,
  And then, I 'm flung away !

Some gaily painted butterfly
  They chase along the road,
Or climbing up a goodly tree
  To view the bird's abode.

I often grow in quiet spot,
  On some great lord's estate ;
And even there my perfume sweet
  Will gratify the great.

But poor or rich, it matters not,
  No difference I trace ;
Yet strive my very best to fill
  Aright my little space.

You see me heaped in many a pile,
  And carried through the street ;
In squalid alley, foul and dim,
  I send my perfume sweet.

And in the wider thoroughfare,
  The passers-by will smile,
As 'mid the dust and glare they scent
  My perfume for awhile.

And dirty little children run
  To catch a fallen spray,
For if they find a flower or two,
  With glee they run away.

And many a weary sufferer
   Will greet me with a smile ;
For pleasant thoughts oft come with
    flowers,
   Their sadness to beguile.

Thus day by day I gather up
   Smiles, laughter, gladness, joy,
And through each season do the work—
   For God doth me employ.

And if I, but a common flower,
   Some holy thoughts can win,
What should you? who hath reason's
    dower,
   Find work to do for Him.

Oh, art thou not encompassed by
   Real work to do for Him—
To aid the souls which Satan bound,
   And help them from their sin ?

What! is your wondrous intellect,
   The power of will and thought,

To pass away like idle dream,
  Which no good work hath wrought?

Up! and be doing, woman, man,
  Find out the Master now,
Then, close to Him, give all thy strength
  To aid the Gospel plough.

————

HAPPY HOME.

HAPPY home, happy home, let the words
    linger,
  Full of sweet melodies, close to our
    heart;
Tracing each thought with love's own
    fairy finger,
  Ne'er from our households we'll let it
    depart.

Happy home, happy home of the earth's
    treasures,
  This is the greatest that e'er could be
    given;

Bringing each day of our heart's deepest
  pleasures,
  Giving to each one a foretaste of
  heaven.

Happy home, happy home, where every
  member
  Takes a full share in the joy, toil, and
  care,
And carries the brightness of May in
  December—
  Then even in trouble we'll never
  despair.

Happy home, happy home, Christ in the
  centre,
  To hallow each hour while passing
  away ;
To open each heart that His own love
  may enter,
  Then home will be dearer through
  every day.

BE THOU FAITHFUL UNTO DEATH, AND I WILL GIVE THEE A CROWN OF LIFE.

Oh, blessed I, oh, blessed thou,
　　What golden link doth bind us;
And, set with many a heavenly gem,
　　What glory hath enshrined us!

The glistening light from Topaz bright
　　Tells of His patient dealing;
And Beryl's gleams each moment seem
　　To aid our deepest feeling.

The Sapphire blue, with heaven's own
　　hue,
　　Shine there as truth most glorious;
Carbuncle's glow, blood-red, doth show
　　That love hath been victorious.

Thus gold and gem united them,
　　That thou and I can't sever;

Unless thy heart take Satan's part,
  The Saviour's thine for ever.

From death came life, and peace from
    strife,
  Good work from self-denial ;
His love to thee, so grand and free,
  Brings joy through every trial.

Thus day by day His truth display,
  And self we'll find retreating
Back, back to him whose presence grim
  Made Eden's bliss so fleeting.

Let patience work, no duty shirk,
  The great I Am will lead thee
Onward each day the conquering way,
  With heavenly manna feed thee.

No earthly crown or great renown,
  His love shall be thy brightness ;
And just His way to perfect day,
  Then glistening robe of whiteness.

HIS FACE UNVEILED.

Written after reading a sermon by A. Brown, of Bow.

LORD,
Let us see Thy face of love
Beaming on us from above;
Chasing every sigh and tear,
Lifting every doubt and fear;
Winning us to follow Thee
In that love light, full and free.
So each day we grow in grace,
As we see Thy unveiled face.

Lord,
Thy holy face we'd see,
That from evil we may flee;
Yearn for purity within,
Shrink from every touch of sin;
See Thy human nature true,
Learn what thou wouldst have us do;
Strong will be our growth in grace,
Seeing that unveiled face.

Lord,
Thy face when it is sad
We would see to make us glad ;
Glad to know that Thou dost share
Every burden we must bear ;
All our sorrow then will be
Working good to us by Thee ;
Truly we shall grow in grace
When we see that unveiled face.

Lord,
Dare we ever ask to see
Thine own face in agony?
See the woe that sin there wrought,
See the victory dearly bought,
See Thee more than Conqueror now
With the blood drops on Thy brow ;
Deeply shall we grow in grace
If we see that unveiled face.

Lord,
All sin must hateful be
When Thy dead face we can see ;
See it in the holy calm
Satan had no power to harm ;

With its majesty of peace,
Testifying our release ;
Restful be our growth in grace,
Gazing on that unveiled face.

Lord,
Thy face with radiance bright,
In its resurrection light,
Showing us the victory won,
And the great work fully done,
Nothing left for us to do
But to share the joy with you ;
Glorious be our growth in grace
While we see that unveiled face.

LOOK UP.

LOOK up, although we may not see the
  light that there is shining ;
Look up, for only there is strength to
  keep us from repining.
Look up, until we catch the gleam from
  Jesus' face so glorious,

Look up, for His great love in us shall
    prove at length victorious.
Look up, that we may catch His light as
    clouds when sun is setting;
Look up, that by His peace inwrought
    the soul is kept from fretting.
Look up that there may be revealed the
    truth of love and beauty;
When we look up there shines the light
    on every daily duty.
Look up till life becomes a spring of
    constant growing pleasure,
For God's own love is just the source of
    untold hidden treasure.

A BIRTHDAY WISH.

"The Lord be with thee."

Oh, can I ask a greater gift,
    Or breathe a better prayer,
Than in your thoughts and words and
    ways,
    The Lord may have His share!

Ruling all powers thou dost possess,
   With His expanding grace ;
That in each circumstance of life
   You rightly fill your place.

Giving the Lord the first of all,
   How nobly wilt thou live !
And in the grace that owns thy gifts,
   His love more joy will give.

We know not till the Spirit comes
   What power we have to do,
Even the trifling acts of life,
   With highest aims in view ;

We cannot tell the joy of faith
   Till that joy fill the breast ;
Nor can we know how sweet His peace
   Till His peace we possess.

The joy and peace which come from faith,
   True, simple faith in Him,
Will leave *no void*, for Christ Himself
   Will fill life to the brim.

How full the living waters flow,
   All dross to purge away !
No room for sin to bud and grow—
   The Lord with thee will stay.

Not as a stranger comes and goes,
   Perhaps at eventide ;
But at the daily social meal
   He ever will abide.

Nearer and nearer thou wilt grow,
   As branch unites to vine,
Thought answering thought, heart beat
     with Him,
   Closely as tendrils twine.

And though the everlasting life
   Here only can begin,
And thou must wait a purer world,
   The higher bliss to win ;

Yet even here, how sweet and bright
   The daily life can be !
The promise still stands firm and true :
   The Lord will be with thee.

So let us hail the thirty-first,
  With praise for every grace,
And seek each passing year to be
  More fit to see His face.

THE OTHER SIDE.

O POWER that maketh two hearts one,
O stream which hath no tide,
But deeper, fuller, brighter flows, on to
                    The other side.

O Love which lightens every woe,
As on life's stream we glide,
Thou dost bridge over death itself, safe to
                    The other side.

O Spell, what mystic influence thou,
Which in few hearts abide,
In such deep, tender, clinging strength,
    to reach
                    The other side.

O Bond that binds so closely dear,
That nothing can divide,
But with a purer flame will glow, when on
                 The other side.

O Breath from Him who gave the power,
What joy Thou dost provide
For those who love and look to be, com-
   plete
                 The other side!

O God, whose highest name is Love,
Come, in our hearts abide,
That one in Thee we here may be, and on
                 The other side.

———

NOT WORTHY TO WORK.

Aii, Satan ! what ? you here again,
　You always know where to find me ;
Well, I think I have strength to sustain
　Another small battle with thee.

Don't hurry, don't hurry to-day,
　For your parcel is done up with care,
As if you quite meant to display
　A tempting bit so rich and rare.

Just something to make me consent
　To your verdict, and say 'tis quite
　　right,
That of walking by faith I repent,
　And henceforth I 'll try walking by
　　sight.

Oh, open your parcel, I pray,
　Its contents I must plainly see ;
For so artful and sly is your way,
　You would say black was white to
　　tempt me.

'Tis only suggestions you bring,
  Which might not occur to *my* mind ;
If I think out and reason the thing,
  I shall find them both helpful and
    kind.

Looking back to the past, I must know
  How the time passed with nothing
    to do ;
And the hours dragged heavy and slow,
  While no work that I wished came to
    view.

Well, Satan, I take up your hint,
  And let my thoughts follow the track ;
The trouble and time I'll not stint,
  To answer this artful attack.

I left London with eager delight,
  To dwell in the country so fair,
And drank in each beautiful sight,
  For of blessings I had a large share.

How friends gathered round I well know,
  With actions and words full of love ;

In return I had naught to bestow,
　But thanks to our Father above.

How I welcomed those tracts as a work
　Through which even I might do good !
By thus teaching no one could be hurt,
　For they told them of spiritual food.

I felt knowing of Jesus would be
　The power to put all wrong right ;
How dirt, drink, and vice must then flee
　From those blessed with spiritual
　　sight.

And the Bible-class, yes, I was glad
　To have those girls gather around ;
I was often more hopeful than sad,
　For I prayed that good fruit might
　　abound.

Oh, yes, Satan, I freely confess,
　From all this I was taken away ;

And the trial no mortal can guess,
   How my heart yearned and pleaded
     to stay.

Then to utter good-bye to each friend
   Was such tender and exquisite pain ;
Though many were earnest and true,
   I expected to see them again.

And my heart often aches with desire,
   Once more in that dear spot to be ;
Feelings *come as* if they were inspired
   That my work there is waiting for me.

Now, Satan, I open your wares—
   'Neath these covers and wraps, what
     dost lurk ?
Why the centre bit briefly declares,
   'Tis because I 'm not worthy to work.

Oh, Satan, what trouble you take
   To rub up my bump of conceit ;
But in this, like the " Why," I must make
   Not an instant's delay to defeat.

Not worthy to work ! understand,
   I always unworthy must be
In that work purely noble and grand,
   That takes not one moment to see ;

And unworthy I ever shall be,
   To tell of the love that did give
All those years of the glorious bliss,
   To teach sinful creatures to live.

Tell of patience, so noble and grand,
   That bore contradiction and sneers ;
And with meekness of power did stand
   'Midst the scoff of those foul Roman
     jeers.

Tell of *one* life quite free from all sin,
   Which He lived in the flesh on this
     earth,
Ever ready the weakest to win,
   Till they sought from Him spiritual
     birth.

Can I ever be worthy to plead
   With others to trust in His Word ;
To seek till their souls too may feed
   On the Fountain of Life from the
   Lord ;

Till they learn what *He* came here to
   teach—
   That *this* life may be flooded with
   bliss ;
For *He* brought that pearl within reach—
   Oh, yes, I'm unworthy for this.

So, Satan, you're wasting to-day,
   And useless is all your disguise ;
You may just take your parcel away,
   'Tis, as usual, a packet of lies.

EDUCATION.

I'D crave a little explanation
Of what you mean by Education :

G

Surely it cannot be, my dear,
That, now you move in first - class
    sphere,
You wish to have within your reach
The ready word or well-turned speech ;
    To talk as glib of things at Rome,
    As those you daily see at home ;
Or speak of many a king whose reign
    In France or Italy, Greece or Spain,
    Were marked by some event so great,
    Or how he kept up sumptuous state ;
    How for a mad king they invented
    Those cards, and many have repented
    That ever they beheld the face
    Of king or queen, of knave or ace.
Don't think I 've any inclination
To write a sneer at any station ;
I 've true respect for each and all—
The high and noble, rich or small—
But this is what I most resent,
That in the mass so few 're content ;
    Think of the many in this nation
    So discontented with their station.
Instead of trying with all might

To make their tiny circle bright,
Doing their best each day to give
Some joy to those with whom they live,
    They tread upon their neighbour's
        ground,
    And show surprise because they found
    So many prickly thorns and briars
    To irritate their own desires ;
And civilisation made it worse,
Whether we worship mind or purse,
    So many things are twisted round,
    The trumpet gives uncertain sound,
    Among the rest in consternation,
    Is this high-sounding Education !
Yet often are we made to feel
'Tis like thick varnish over deal,
Not honest polish by the hand—
If 'twas, then we could understand
Whether the wood was good or no,
If fit for use or only show ;
Could trace each mark and fibrous vein.
    But this I earnestly maintain
    That people often make mistake
    With those they think they *educate.*

The word itself aright defined,
Means nurture, discipline of mind;
'Tis something higher, nobler, better
Than all they teach by form or letter;
Not graceful flow of words and prattle,
As if our tongue were doing battle.
      But clasp my hand and we will rise
      To fairer views and brighter skies.
Just think how grand is the foundation
When God begins our education!
How deep He dives within the heart
To sanctify each hidden part!
Lay but our will before His feet
And He will make the work complete.
Then love becomes both pure and holy,
And, though we note the growth but
      slowly,
It grows with every little trial,
Until the power of self-denial
Becomes a clear and well-known part,
Rooted within a Christian's heart;
For deep's the trench where self is laid,
And with humility 'tis paved;
How vanity must slink away

Before the power of Gospel ray,
Not only vanity of station,
Of look or dress or education,
But that of a more subtle kind,
When praise can elevate the mind ;
And like to Nebuchadnezzar's feeling
A gladness o'er our senses stealing,
Till satisfaction sits in state,
Before we know she's in the gate.
    I do not mean that sweet sensation
    When God shows us His approbation,
    After sore struggle and prayer, maybe,
    When grace has gained the victory ;
Nor do I mean when one most dear,
Whose deathless love is mixed with
    fear
Lest we should say or do a wrong,
Knowing our enemy's so strong,
That if we leave the smallest place
Unguarded, he will find the space ;
    But when a loved one gives us praise,
    'Tis food to last for many days,
    And God permits us such to eat—
    The manna was itself most sweet ;

Then every day as God works more,
So all our pleasure will be pure ;
If we enjoy because He gives it,
We shall not cloy when we receive it ;
Then sweet content will fill the part
That's built for her in every heart ;
It keeps the lips from many a grumble,
And guards the feet from many a stumble ;
Opens our eyes to joys unknown,
That thickly cluster round our home.

   And if we have this grand foundation,
   We each may build our education.
   Art ! build thy edifice most fair,
   With pinnacles and arches rare—
   Picture the galleries with food
   For mind and eye in all that's good ;
   And music ! let the joyful sound
   Of melody float all around ;
   Measure the heavens, name each star,
   Learn of the countries near and far,
   The mountains grand, the cedars tall,
   The desert sand, the waterfall ;
   Class every flower that gems the ground
   And beautifies this earth around ;

As time and wealth and health are
    given,
Each day, more fit for earth and
    heaven,
Should we be sure that we inherit
A double portion of the Spirit—
It then will give us small vexation
If we lack earthly Education.

CAST THY BURDEN ON THE LORD.

May 31st.

EVERY bit of my burden,
    O Lord, I'd give to Thee ;
I crave for that grand liberty
    By which Thou dost make free.

Every bit of my burden,
    I would not keep a share,
But casting it before Thy Cross,
    I'd leave it in Thy care.

Every bit of my burden,
   For I would walk upright,
With joy fulfil my daily work
   Completely in Thy sight.

Every bit of my burden,
   Or it will mar my speed,
And spoil the power of heart and
     mind
   Which every day doth need.

Every bit of my burden,
   No clouds want I between ;
But love, and joy, and peace to flow
   From Thee the great Unseen.

Every bit of my burden,
   Then dark despair will hide
Its puckered brow and dismal look
   Far from Thy wounded side.

Every bit of my burden,
   And I shall be quite free
From all the bondage Satan tries
   Each day to cast round me.

Every bit of my burden,
  Lord ! is it really true
That I should live without a care,
  And all should fall on you?

Oh, send Thy Holy Spirit!
  That I may clearly see
My every care is truly Thine,
  And Love, Thy Love's for me.

COL. i. 19 ; ii. 9.

FOR it pleased the Father, oh wonderful thought,
How free the salvation for sinners Christ
  bought ;
For it pleased the Father, and glad
  should we be
To rejoice in the goodness which thus
  set us free;

For it pleased the Father who *all* things
    does well,
That in Jesus our Saviour, all fulness
    should dwell ;
For it pleased the Father, in Christ to
    complete
A safe narrow pathway for stumbling
    feet ;
For it pleased the Father, whose full
    name is Love,
To hold out the hand-clasp from
    heaven above ;
For it pleased the Father, the weakest
    to win,
By lifting the barrier to let them all in ;
For it pleased the Father a body to give,
Prepared where the Godhead in Jesus
    could live ;
For it pleased the Father that bright
    crimson stain
Should sprinkle the pathway for deaf,
    blind, and lame ;
For it pleased the Father, yet how can
    we tread

On that holy ground where the Saviour
    hath bled ?
For it pleased the Father, and Satan
    must feel
He was but permitted to bruise the
    Lord's heel ;
For it pleased the Father, then loud let
    us sing,
And grow in the knowledge of Jesus our
    King;
Each day in the sunshine of love, we can
    tell
That in Jesus our Saviour God's fulness
    doth dwell.

JUST AS THOU WILT.

JUST as Thou wilt, Lord,
    Sickness or health ;
Just as Thou wilt, Lord,
    Poverty, wealth ;

Just as Thou wilt, Lord,
  If I'm only Thine,
To serve Thee on earth,
  Then in glory to shine.

Just as Thou wilt, Lord,
  Teach me the way
Daily to seek Thee,
  To serve and obey.
Just as Thou wilt, Lord,
  Shall be all the rest,
For well do I know
  That Thy way is the best.

Just as Thou wilt, Lord,
  Live Thou in me ;
Happy my life, Lord,
  Joyous and free,
To one so unworthy,
  If grace be but given
To tread the bright pathway
  From earth up to heaven.

Just as Thou wilt, Lord,
  Satan is strong ;
Stretch out Thy hand, Lord,
  To keep me from wrong ;
And when he is tempting
  Me to the broad way,
Lord, send me Thy Spirit
  For fear I should stray.

Just as Thou wilt, Lord,
  Make my will Thine ;
In every trial
  I ne'er shall repine.
My faith will be steadfast,
  And firm to the end ;
The love that has bought me
  Will always defend.

ALMOST SAVED.

ALMOST saved, almost saved !
  Sadly the words ring out to me,

Like the boom of a gun from a sinking
    ship,
  Sounding over the stormy sea,
              Almost saved.

Almost saved, the land so nigh
  That loving ones could clearly hear,
In the midst of the roar of the troubled
    sea,
  That wailing, piercing cry of fear,
              Almost saved.

Almost saved, as still they see
  Those twinkling lights along the shore ;
Which so tauntingly gleam to despair-
    ing eyes
  So near the well-known cottage door,
              Almost saved.

Almost saved, some tiny sin
  Tempted them with its smiling face ;
Till it led far away from the narrow
    path,
  Deeper, deeper into disgrace,
              Almost saved.

Almost saved, they thought no wrong
  Just to step off from God's straight
    way ;
There could be no harm, 'twas done all
  around,
  Yet those poor souls would have to
    say,
          Almost saved.

Almost saved, 'twas angel eyes
  They thought would lead them on the
    road ;
And they deemed it right to follow the
  track
  Which led away from God's abode,
          Almost saved.

Almost saved, a little more
  Of wrestling with the tempter's power;
Had they sought for His aid, with a
  firmer faith,
  Never would come that gloomy hour,
          Almost saved.

A BEE'S SOLILOQUY.

"If no honey, then wax."

O Joy, I can't find thee to-day,
Come patience, let us plod away
　　　And stop my moaning;
O sweet content, where canst thou be?
Well industry, I'll bide with thee
　　　To cease from groaning.
Ah, praise with thee the woods should
　　ring,
But perseverance help shall bring,
　　　Lest work should tire.
And gratitude, hast thou too fled?
Then faith shall fill the place instead
　　　And aid desire.
I fain my heart with peace would fill,
Humility abide here still,
　　　I'll not stop growing.
O Bee, could I but learn of thee
And use each opportunity
　　　Of God's bestowing,

Until I really see His love
Shine clear on me from Christ above,
And my glad heart can send back love
    Fresh, full, and glowing.

TAKE NO THOUGHT FOR THE MORROW.

ONE day at a time, one day at a time,
    How sweetly those words can tell
That the wisdom and love *are* all Divine
    Which measured my strength so well.

One day at a time, one day at a time,
    'Tis surely enough for me ;
If the light from Thy face on each duty
    shine,
    It must bring me nearer Thee.

One day at a time, one day at a time,
    There's plenty of work to do ;
But the work which I crave must all be
    Thine—
    I would labour with the few.

H

One day at a time, one day at a time,
 Take my powers and let them be
Made pure by Thy love, till all combine
 To lead a soul to Thee.

One day at a time, one day at a time,
 My strength with *Thy joy* now fill ;
Let a pulse of Thy life make my own
  sublime,
 As I work into God's will.

One day at a time, one day at a time,
 In simple trust I say
That the wisdom and love are all Divine
 Which guideth me through each day.

———

BIRTHDAY WISHES.

May 31st.

Now what shall I wish you ? a full self-
  surrender
 To Him who hath borne all thy
  sorrow and sin,

And proveth Himself a completed
    Redeemer   [win?
By giving the power each victory to

Now what shall I wish you? a peace
    ever flowing
  Through the water and blood from
    His spear-riven side ;
His peace which *Thy trials* shall aid in
    the growing,
  Then *nothing* shall harm thee whate'er
    may betide.

Now what shall I wish you? a trust so
    resplendent,
  Just wedged between mountains of
    faith in the Lord,
No thing can disturb, 'tis securely trans-
    cendent,   [Word?
  Because the foundation is built on His

Now what shall I wish you? a faith so
    clear-sighted,
  That invisible things in their power
    are near?

Then the thickest of clouds will not find
    thee benighted,
    For Christ is the compass by which
    thou wilt steer.

Now what shall I wish you? a love deep
    and glowing
    To worship the Lord in the strength
    of thy soul,
And finding Him ready, His own love
    bestowing,
    Engulfing thy heart where no tide
    doth control?

Now what shall I wish you? a joy full
    of brightness
    To dwell in your heart as you live
    through each day?
Then the cares and the trials of earth
    will find lightness
    As you consciously walk in the
    strait, narrow way.

Now what shall I wish you? a dignified
    meekness,
    As you walk on this earth with His
       calm in thine heart,
May the praises of men or their blame
    find no weakness,
    Nor Satan get room to discharge a
       swift dart.

Now what shall I wish you? why, bless-
    ings unnumbered,
    That circles a home, where the souls
       learn to see
That *true* work for the Master is free
    and uncumbered;
    And this work I ask Him for thee
       and for me.

THIS SPACE TO LET.

On the blank page of a letter these words were
written—*This space to Let.*

THIS space to let, come, let me try
Some thoughts to borrow, beg, or buy;

This empty space wherewith to fill,
To do it well is past my skill.

This space to let, now oft might we
Write this above our memory ;
So many blessings are forgot,
So dolefully we bear our lot.

This space to let, 'twas never meant
That we should rest with this content ;
But strive to have no empty space,
With good work filling up each place.

This space to let, God grant that we
May do His work with energy ;
For taint of sin, remember, yet
Clings close around each space to let.

This space to let, soon Satan's eye
The smallest vacant space will spy,
And quickly send some evil thought
To fill the space he never bought.

This space to let, O Saviour dear,
Send to us, from Thy own bright sphere,
Thy Spirit good our hearts to fill
With love unto Thy blessed will.

That every space may bear its fruit,
From Thine own self its spring and root ;
Then we 'll not murmur with regret,
Would I had left no Space to Let.

———

ALL ON THE SURFACE.

ALL on the surface, and no thing beneath,
Like a vine full of leaves, or no sword in
 the sheath ;
All on the surface, the show and parade,
With their bows, smiles, and compli-
 ments, all ready made;
All on the surface, the coat must fit well,
Or society's frown at the culprit will tell ;
All on the surface must follow the code
Of fashion, in each thing be quite *à la
 mode ;*

All on the surface, the cut of the vest
Must be perfect! no matter what heart's
    in the breast—
It may swell high with passion, or turn
    cold with hate,
It may revel in envy at other's estate.
But if all on the surface be calm and
    serene,
Who heeds any tempers that dwell there
    unseen?

LIVE TO GOD.

No matter where should be my lot—
Be it a palace or a cot;
To throw the shuttle, turn the clod,
Be this my motto—Live to God!

If it be wealth with grand estate,
Or toil from early morn till late,
Or tremble at a despot's nod,
Be this my motto—Live to God!

To never have one moment's ease,
Or never do one thing I please,
Or look for rest but 'neath the sod,
Still be my motto—Live to God!

Though every day should bring much
  care,
And great the burden I must bear,
I'll humbly bow beneath the rod,
And keep the motto—Live to God!

SYMPATHY.

ALTHOUGH I am a stranger,
  Yet how pleasant it will be,
If like a gleam of sunshine
  I brought comfort unto thee.

For I know you must be weary,
  So tired of sitting still;
While hands and feet are wanting
  To move just as you will.

You see so many duties,
 And wish each one to do ;
To sit still is so irksome,
 Almost too much for you ;

And I can just feel with you,
 I know how great the loss
Not to have power to move about,
 That is a daily cross.

Yet liberty is given,
 There are three paths to choose ;
And 'tis my past experience
 I give for you to use.

First, I could be rebellious,
 And say it was not right
That I should just be put aside
 From work that was delight.

And why should other people
 Have power to come and go ?
While I in weary pain should count
 The hours that drag so slow.

And oft my mind was fretted
  In thinking of my cross ;
And many an hour I wasted
  In pondering o'er my loss.

A second way was open :
  I could sit in sullen mood,
Bearing the great monotony,
  Taking my daily food ;

The done could not be undone,
  All my talk would be in vain ;
If I was fated here to sit
  I had better not complain.

But a third way yet was offered,
  Very narrow to my view ;
And patience must be taken up,
  If I would travel through ;

Self must be placed in bondage,
  And grace must have full power
To lop off every useless twig
  That sprouteth any hour ;

I must never put a limit
　To weariness or pain,
But rest upon the promise given
　That loss would yet be gain ;

Believe and trust, trust and believe,
　God doeth all things well ;
The why must be put on one side,
　What 's best to me He 'll tell.

And as the weeks thus lengthen out
　To months, and on to years,
How graciously He helpeth me
　Through all my doubts and fears.

Each day He giveth to me power
　To live within the day ;
Each morning He is waiting still,
　To help me on His way.

What He has for to-morrow's strength,
　That need not trouble me ;
It may be light upon a path
　I shall delight to see.

The clouds at any moment's time
May let the sunshine through ;
I only need to know His Will,
And seek that Will to do.

———

WITH A GIFT.

" Gold, gold, gold, gold,
Bright and yellow, hard and cold,
Molten, graven, hammered, and rolled,
Gold, gold, gold, gold."
HOOD.

THUS said the man whose ready wit
Could make the lines so quaintly fit,
That reading was a pleasure.
Whose subtle brain could twist and
turn
To use the words which others spurn,
Such wit's a boundless treasure.

But my poor brain can not compare
With such keen power, rich and rare,
I could not write a sonnet.

For difference vast be understood,
'Twixt him whose head could own a
    Hood,
    And one who wears a bonnet.

Now to commemorate this day,
And make its memory live for aye,
    I send this golden present.
Though small its worth, thou 'll not re-
    fuse,
Often the little gift to use,
    With recollection pleasant.

The stars and stripes thereon engraved,
May illustrate the light and shade
    To us in this life given.
So near each other yet apart,
Like joy and sorrow in a heart,
    When pressing on to heaven.

O happy thought for us to know
'Tis stars above, and stripes below,
    If we believe the Word;

And looking forward clearly see
An endless, bright eternity,
    For those who love the Lord.

But now my earnest wish shall be,
That when this gift is used by thee,
    'Twill always strengthen right.
That goodness, honesty, and truth,
Those sure, safe guides to age and
    youth,
    May aid thee in life's fight.

O Pen, how wonderful thy power
For ill or good in one short hour,
    Should gifted mortal use it.
Few of thy strokes it takes to make
A vast amount of cash at stake,
    Your trust, should friend abuse it.

How great our trial is none can tell,
Save Him who doeth all things well,
    And knows our one desire :

That we like gold, when sorely tried,
May come out clean and purified,
   By passing through His fire.

————

AN APPEAL FROM A SICK-BED.

SISTER, turn from sin and sorrow,
   From all the tempting paths of guilt ;
Come to Him who gently calls you,
   For your soul His blood was spilt.

Sister, turn from guilty pleasure,
   Though hard the struggle, great the
     pain ;
Come to Him who now will help you,
   And take away your sin and shame.

Sister, turn from Satan's whisper,
   That 'tis too late for such as you ;
Come to Him who has the power,
   Now to create your heart anew.

Sister, turn ; our hands are open
    To welcome yours with loving clasp ;
Our hearts in tenderness are yearning,
    To rescue you from Satan's grasp.

Sister, turn ; no looks of scorning
    Will Christians dare on you to cast ;
But humbly strive to help the erring,
    To turn from all the bitter past.

Looking back through many ages,
    See, there a crowd is pressing on ;
In the midst a helpless woman,
    Whom they regard with bitter scorn.

Placing her before the Saviour—
    How great the sin which makes her
      feel—
She cannot meet His gaze so holy—
    Nor dare she as a suppliant kneel.

Droopingly she stands before Him,
    With downcast eyes and heaving
      breast ;

How deep she feels her degradation,
  By words can never be expressed.

Scarce she hears those clamorous voices,
  Each eager for an answer now ;
" Rabbi, Master," so says Moses,
  " Hear us, tell us, what sayest thou ? "

Scarce she heeds the sudden silence
  Which follows on the Master's voice ;
Or her poor brow would cease its
    throbbing,
  And her sad heart would then rejoice.

Hark ! swelling on the solemn stillness,
  No harsh rebuke comes sounding o'er ;
But gentlest, tenderest words of pity :
  " Daughter, go and sin no more."

Oh ! yes, methinks till life's last hour,
  Though battling with temptations
    sore,   [power—
Those precious words ne'er lost their
  " Daughter, go and sin no more."

TO A. B.

FAR away from the Master,
  My dear, how can that be?
For is it not a glorious fact,
  He's never far from Thee.

Far away from the Master,
  I cannot think 'tis so;
But just some earthly mists which rise
  To keep thy spirits low.

Oh, think how near was Mary,
  How earnest she did plead:
Sir, tell me where you laid Him,
  That I may go with speed.

How very near the Master,
  When they cried out with fear,
In the misty gloom, before them loom,
  A spirit coming near.

How near in early morning,
  When He stood on the shore,

It was not till the wondrous draught
 That John knew Him once more.

Near to them was the Master,
 Discoursing by the way;
But eyes were held, though lips did
 cry,
 Abide with us I pray.

And are not our eyes holden?
 We cannot understand,
He ever waits in love so strong,
 To take us by the hand.

Though Satan's ever ready
 To make our doubts seem true,
With art together he ties our I's,
 And turns them into U.

U ought not to have done this,
 And that U ought to do;
His great keynote's a spurious one,
 'Tis U, and U, and U.

Yet often do we listen,
    And then we look within ;
Till U and I such a burden prove,
    That we see nought but sin.

And is not this our failing,
    Ah, well does Satan know
If Christ were ruling *all* our thoughts,
    Each doubt and fear would go.

So you and I will trust Him,
    Then will He draw us near,
Till faith shall clasp His nail-scarred
    hand,
    And love cast out all fear.

BOYS WITHOUT SOULS.

Suggested by a Conversation with Mr. C.

GOING home to my lodging weary,
    My spirits low and sad,
As I thought of the little progress
    I made with each ragged lad.

Then I knelt before Our Father,
  Who doeth all things well,
And prayed that His Holy Spirit
  Might soon in each young heart dwell.

But my tired head scarce rested
  On the pillow soft and clean,
When away my thoughts were drifted
  In a strange and vivid dream.

I was treading the well-known pathway,
  Each house and shop I knew ;
And had often counted the paces
  Which would bring the school in view.

Soon I reached the well-known doorway;
  My watch, thought I, is wrong;
I 'm too early by this deep silence—
  No scuffle, or voice, or song !

I slowly went to the schoolroom,
  The scene there kept me mute ;
For each lad in my class kept silent,
  No chuckle or rough salute.

I knelt, for the bell was ringing,
    And gazed with eager eyes,
As they bent in a measured movement,
    Which added to my surprise.

I was seated with open Bible,
    And tried each face to scan ;
I wanted some clue to this silence
    Before the lesson began.

Why, Bob, Tom, Jack, William, Harry,
    What's the matter with all of you ?
Then each head was lifted in silence,
    While horror thrilled me through.

No gleam of defiance or mischief,
    No saucy smile was there,
But a glassy cold and senseless gaze ;
    Then my heart sank in despair.

I wanted my boys to be quiet,
    Each lesson learnt aright ;
Obedience to every order
    Would have given me delight.

I had wrestled with earnest longing,
  The narrow path to tread,
And prayed that each youthful scholar
  Might in that same path be led.

But these soulless looks awakened
  A new and startling thought—
Was I wrong in my way of teaching,
  Had all *self* been where it ought?

So I cried aloud in my terror:
  O Christ, Thou art the goal;
Let me bear the burden of patience,
  But restore each boy his soul.

I awoke, for the sun was shining
  On me with brilliant beam;   [ing,
My heart throbbed with true thanksgiv-
  That it only was a dream.

But what a lasting lesson
  That vivid dream has taught,
An ever-living blessing,
  To all my power of thought.

Each boy stands on the merit
   Of Christ's great work for me,
Each soul bought by the Ransom,
   Whose power can make us free.

But time does pass so quickly,
   My class is quiet now ;
Not with that horrid silence,
   For thought sits on each brow.

Tom's eyes still have a twinkle
   Of mischief, in the blue ;
And William's lost their sullen look,
   Though almost black in hue ;

Bob's grey orbs often glisten,
   For Christ is all my theme ;
I feel more tender o'er them
   Since that vivid, dreadful dream.

So with much prayer to Jesus,
   I help them fight all sin,
And expect no reformation
   From *without*, but from *within*.

SORROW.

HUSH, tread gently, Death's dark arrow
    Has struck here—our flower is dead ;
Gone to bloom in heavenly mansions,
    Where no tear of sorrow 's shed.

Oh, how dark and strange the curtain,
    Which hides the cause of this deep
      woe ;
Why pass again through troubled water,
    See another dear one go?

Were the tendrils *too* clinging,
    Which tiny lips and hands had wove?
Were our fond hearts their garlands
      flinging
    Too close round our treasure trove?

Had the precious baby prattle
    Deadened higher, heavenlier sound?
In all the fight of earthly battle,
    Were we getting too earth-bound?

Thou who knows our hearts' deep feeling,
   And works all things by *Thine* own
     will ;   [ing,
In our breasts, like heaven's chime peal-
   May we hear Thy—Peace be still.

With hushed lips and hearts o'erflowing,
   Touched with Thy great love to us ;
We find our life near to Thee growing,
   Trial purifies us thus.

MY FRIEND.

To dear Mr. Fox.

My Friend! there's magic in the words,
   More sweet than siren's song ;
They touch the heart's deep tender
     chords,
   And, as they float along,
'Tis like some lovely mountain rill,
Whose silvery notes are never still.

My Friend! whose love we fully trust,
    Deep, tender, firm, and true;
'Tis no spasmodic sudden gush,
    But strong and ever new,
Up-springing like a lovely flower,
Made perfect by the sun and shower.

My Friend! the link that binds our
    hearts
    Was never forged on earth,
So finely wrought in all its parts,
    Must be of heavenly birth;
From Him whose spirit can bestow
A gift without a flaw to grow.

My Friend! how can we praise His
    name,
    Who caused us to be
So wonderful in mind and frame,
    Yet with a *will* so *free*,
That we can use it any way,
And through Christ's love, *God's Will*
    obey.

My Friend! what will the Lord reveal,
　As we shall know Him more?
What strength of spirit-life unseen,
　That we may Him adore,
And know a joy that has no end,
The bliss wrapped up in a real friend.

———

NEW YEAR, 1879.

A HAPPY New Year
　To all who are here,
Though sorrow has steeped us in gloom;
　Yet since Jesus died,
　On the cross crucified,
There's a light on the path to the tomb.

　Our dear one has gone,
　Our loss we must mourn,
Her place here will know her no more;
　Those sweet gentle ways
　From infancy's days,
How deeply the loss we deplore.

The tears dim our eyes,
As we gaze on the skies,
And think, Is she with her dear child,
In union sweet,
At the Saviour's feet,
In bliss, free from sin, undefiled?

But yet while we grieve,
That us she would leave
To fight out the battle with sin ;
We hope to press on
In the path she has gone,
And a like crown of glory to win.

When that time shall come,
May the welcome, Well done !
Fall with rapturous bliss on each heart ;
As we enter the home,
Pressing on round the throne,
Never more, never more will we part.

————

O GENTLE FRIEND.

O GENTLE friend, whom suffering hath
  refined,
Till self seems banished from the pre-
  cincts of thy mind.
O gentle friend, whose words and looks
  breathe blessed calm,
As if thy spirit had been bathed in
  Gilead's balm.
O gentle friend, to me though art like
  summer eve,
O'er which the deep hushed silence of
  our God doth breathe.
O gentle friend, thou art linked close
  with peaceful things—
A tranquil lake bathed in the light that
  moonbeam flings,
A landscape fair on some light, soft,
  grey day,
A rippling sea o'er which the sunbeams
  play,

A calm, deep sleep, when care is quite
 laid by,
Or that full peace when Christ Himself
 is nigh ;
O gentle friend, my nature seems so full
 of strife,
Strong wishes, deep desires, wrestling
 for their active life ;
And hence thy peaceful calm so beautiful appears,
Although its roots were bathed in bitter
 tears.

MY SISTER.

SEVEN winters' snows have come,
 Seven springs to flowers gave birth,
Seven summers' ardent sun,
 And seven autumns blest the earth.

Long though swift the time has been,
 As each season passed away ;

Pain and weariness oft reigned,
   Clouding many a night and day.

Time brings no oblivion draught
   To dim the heart's deep joy or woe ;
No adamantine wall to check
   The strong full tide of memory's flow.

Nor would I chase one thought away,
   Which bringeth aught of thee to mind,
Thy look or gesture, words or ways,
   Most loving, gentle, true, and kind.

Fondly loved, and deeply mourned,
   As weeks and months and years roll
     by,
My heart for thee still truly yearns,
   And oft I wish that thou wert nigh.

We miss thee in our daily walk,
   We miss thee at the quiet eve ;
Thy gentle smile and loving talk
   All gone, and we are left to grieve.

K

And yet we strive to bear our pain,
   In faith to bow and kiss the rod,
To feel our loss is but thy gain,
   That thou art safe in heaven with God.

Thou art not lost, but gone before—
   This thought alone can help our woe,
And teach us hope to meet once more,
   Or check the bitter tears which flow.

Yes! blessed are the pure in heart,
   Are words which fell from lips Divine,
And as we read, though big tears start,
   We love to think that bliss is thine.

MRS. TURNBULL.

GONE to the eternal home,
   Where angels' songs are sounding;
Gone to join the heavenly choir,
   Jehovah's throne surrounding.

Gone to everlasting life,
   Free from all pain and sorrow;

Free from daily care and needs,
    That here waits each to-morrow.

Gone to know the wondrous bliss
    No mortal can discover;
Her soul and spirit now are free
    From cumbrous earthly cover.

Her spirit now is with the just,
    With joy her face is beaming;
She wears a robe of righteousness,
    With gems her crown is gleaming.

Gone, gone, gone, still echoes here,
    Though she has gone to glory;
And we with many a sigh and tear,
    Make her loss all our story.

We want her here, we want her now,
    And every want feels double;
Her loving care still sweeter seems
    In all our daily trouble.

The home is blank, each room feels dark,
   In which no sun is shining ;
Oh ! how we miss her loving self,
   So precious, so refining.

Her spirit was so pure and true,
   So quick each want relieving ;
She never seemed to take from us—
   We always were receiving.

Pleasant her words as rippling rill,
   Her looks with love were glowing ;
Constant her work for others' good,
   Unselfish wisdom showing.

But now she is so far away,
   And we so sad and lonely—
'Twas her bright presence, day by day,
   That made our home so homely.

And yet, she may not be so far,
   For true love cannot sever ;
The link though broken reunites,
   The parting's not for ever.

And as the time rolls on apace,
   Will not the veil grow thinner?
The shade that parts our spirits now
   Let through some heavenly glimmer?

May not we near and nearer grow,
   Till death's bridge spans the river;
Then in that golden city meet,
   To part no more for ever.

Then in the light of Christ the Lamb,
   We'll learn to know the reason,
Why through this trial of deepest woe
   We struggled for a season.

THE BOY.

HENRY EDWIN DARLEY.

20th February, 1890.

FIVE years the Master lent him,
   A sunbeam in the home;
And then to heaven called him,
   Boy now to " Jedee " come.

All ready he to leave us
　　For that bright home on high :
" Mama, boy go to Jedee,
　　Yight up into the kie."

His spirit needs no cleansing,
　　For Jesus' blood had bought
That bright young soul to love Him,
　　And praise Him as we ought.

Our boy knew Jesus loved him,
　　His faith, unmixed with sin,
Could hear the Saviour calling
　　The little one to Him.

No time had worldly fetters
　　To rivet on a sin ;
No time had Satan's subtleties
　　To make boy foul within.

But clear, and fresh, and holy,
　　Stamped with the Master's grace,
Boy could look up to Jesus here,
　　And see Him face to face.

Oh, do not think upon him
　　As boy cold, white and dead ;
Bind not thy thoughts to earthly clay,
　　As bitter tears you shed.

But let thy tears be prisms
　　That they may bring to thee
Some of the light from rainbow bright,
　　Which now the boy doth see.

Till resting on thy Spirit,
　　Crown like the martyrs wore,
Of glowing light from glory bright,
　　Where boy has gone before.

Oh, dignity of knowing
　　That God did grant to thee
A gift so worth his taking back
　　While it was pure and free.

And though this mystic glory
　　Is through heart-sorrow bought,
Oh, could you offer to your Lord
　　Of that which cost thee nought.

But every tear of anguish,
  And every sigh of pain,
Will in the end bear richest crop
  Of heaven's golden grain.

For when in that pure brightness
  The boy once more shall rest,
In joyous love and beauty bright
  Upon thy faithful breast,

Thou wilt not grudge the sorrow
  Of all the weary years ;
The empty place beside the hearth,
  Or joys that passed in tears ;

But depth of joyous gladness,
  That here we cannot know,
Will fill thy being with a bliss
  God can alone bestow.

Then through the great for-ever
  Thou and the boy shall live ;
Thou with the boy, the boy with thee,
  Shall endless praises give.

LINES ON THE DEATH OF AN AFFECTIONATE SISTER-IN-LAW,

Who died 30th April, 1871.

ANOTHER link is broken,
  Another loved one gone ;
Our God the word hath spoken,
  And we are left to mourn.

Sad, sad, our tears are falling,
  Deep, deep, our sorrow now ;
She 's gone beyond recalling,
  We to the blow must bow.

And must we bear this sorrow ?
  And must we bear this pain ?
Nor look for brighter morrow
  To meet her once again ?

Is there no gleam of lightness
  To help us on our way ?
No touch of heavenly brightness
  To cheer us while we stay ?

Yes, thanks to God our Saviour—
    Who triumphed o'er the tomb—
Whose Spirit's gracious favour
    Can cheer our deepest gloom.

If He but grant His Spirit
    To teach us how to live,
We'll bless each joy or sorrow
    His gracious hand may give.

May this deep trouble bring us
    Closer unto His Cross :
His Spirit work within us,
    Bring gain from this our loss.

Thus day by day we'll journey
    Nearer unto that land,
Where waiting are our loved ones
    'Midst God's own chosen band.

LINES ON THE DEATH OF A BELOVED NIECE,

Who died, 26th September, 1871.

LITTLE Annie is no more,
All her pain and suffering o'er ;
God has called her far away
To the realms of endless day.

Wipe those tears ! now, kneel and pray !
Thank the gracious Lord this day,
That she 's taken safely home,
Where no pain can ever come.

Thank the Lord ! to you who gave
Strength to nurse her for the grave ;
Think how great your joy will be
When your darling you shall see—

Not in weakness, suffering, pain,
But amid the angelic train ;
With the chosen Lambs of God,
Washed and saved by Jesus' blood.

Praise Him! who to us has given
Such a glorious hope of Heaven;
May we meet each loved one there,
And eternal glory share.

Though our little Annie's dead,
Still no bitter tears we'll shed;
But in humble trust now say,
God has taken her away.

———

TO MARY.

LITTLE Mary, daisy bright,
Art thou gone to realms of light?
Few the steps upon life's road
Which thy tiny feet have trod.

Few the troubles which have pressed,
On thy little infant breast—
Troubles which to each one come,
As they tread the pathway home.

Thou art mourning, Mary dear,
That thy darling is not here,
But she's garnered safe above,
Safe within those Arms of love.

I seem to see her all the while
With father's eyes and mother's smile,
Which brightened all her baby face,
Adding to beauty such a grace.

No more she'll need thy tender care,
No more in household joys have share,
No clinging touch of tiny hands
Will seem to strengthen love's sweet
    bands.

Well I know thy tender heart,
Deeply it will feel this dart;
Wrung with anguish, torn with pain,
You scarce can think thy loss her gain.

Scarce can feel it is true love
By which thy darling was removed;

Taking from thy life such joy,
From thy hands such sweet employ.

How much you long to clasp her now,
And kiss her lips, and smooth her brow!
No joy could be so great on earth—
Your heart would hardly hold its mirth.

But now your heart is full of grief,
No thought can bring the least relief;
This cloud sits heavy on thy brow,
All earth looks sad and gloomy now.

Yet Christ is gazing now on thee,
His love Divine thy needs can see;
He feels your grief and knows your
    pain,
And He can make this grief your gain.

In tender love He called thy flower,
And gathered it this wintry hour—
So deep His love to each one's soul,
He gave Himself to make us whole.

THOUGHTS OF MR. FOX.

*Our precious friend, thank God we were
permitted to know him.*

HE is gone, he is gone, how the echo
   surrounds us,
  It glides through the sunshine, it
   floats in the air ;
The rustling leaves do but carry them
   round us,
  While hearts bowed in grief that
   same echo declare.

He is gone, he is gone, oh! the gap in our
   pleasure,
  Our words seem too feeble when trying to tell
How his love used to flow like a tide
   without measure,
  And sympathy's touch seemed to act
   like a spell.

He is gone, he is gone, but we would
    not recall him
  To share in our pleasure, and comfort
    our pain ;
Or check sin and vice which would
    cower before him,
  For we know that our loss unto him
    must be gain.

He is gone, he is gone, to the Saviour
    who bought him,
  He knows the deep bliss of faith
    crowned by sight ;
And though for his life with heart
    groans we besought Him,
  We must own it is well, for *God*
    always does right.

He is gone, he is gone, but his words we
    remember—
  "Not me, but the Master," he'd say
    with a smile.

When some loving deed had made
    heart and voice tender,
  He strove from that subject our
    thoughts to beguile.

He is gone, he is gone, but his deeds
    glow and brighten,
  As thought takes the draught brought
    by memory's knell ;
So many sad hearts did his kindnesses
    lighten,
  And will not his welcome be, Thou
    hast done well !

He is gone, he is gone, yet he beckoneth
    to us
  To keep the same path, and press on
    with the few,
Oh, may God by His grace in the
    Saviour renew us,
  With single-eyed faith that same
    path to pursue.

He is gone, he is gone, to the heart rest
    for ever,
  Where peace of the soul is not
    ruffled by strife,
Where Christ is the centre from which
    nought can sever,
  The joy and the glory, the life and
    the light.

He is gone, he is gone, but the heart-
    link remaineth,
  For though he is lost to material
    sight,
Is there not subtle power which ever
    sustaineth,   [unite?
  That spirit with spirit may often

So we weep for the loss, yet hope's
    whisper reminds us,
  That we *all* are one who are found
    in the Lord ;
With His spirit to guide, may each pass-
    ing day find us,   [cord.
  Bound closer together by sympathy's

TO MRS. EMMA ROAN,

On hearing of her brother's death, 28th July, 1885.

I KNOW your heart is very sad,
 How deep its sorrow none can tell ;
You hoped for tidings bright and glad,
 While death was pealing forth its
  knell.

How deep the mystery of that blow,
 And heart-felt struggle seem to cry,
That wife and loved ones need him so,
 We're tempted sore to ask the *Why.*

Hush, hush, sad heart ! weep on awhile,
 On earth no reason can you trace ;
Wait till in heaven you see his smile,
 And feel once more his glad embrace.

Now you must mourn and weep and
 sigh,
 And Jesus shares in all your grief ;
In His good time He'll show you why
 This sickness met with no relief.

So hard, so hard, we mourning cry,
  To place our dear ones 'neath the sod ;
But solemn sounds both far and nigh,
  " Be still and know that I am God."

And as time's balm with softening touch
  Gives us the power on Him to rest,
We 'll cease to sorrow over much,
  And humbly say—God's way is best.

———

THINKING OF LIZZIE OGILVIE'S PURE LIFE AND EARLY DEATH.

" Consider the lilies how they grow, they toil not, neither do they spin."

Not Solomon in all his prime, was ever
    half so fair,
Though purple rich, fine linen white, and
    costly gems were there ;
And gold, the bright, pure, yellow gold,
    became of little worth,
Silver was such a trifling thing, like
    common clods of earth ;

And peace fell on the nations round, by
    God's great mercy given—
Not all of this was half so fair as Lizzie,
    gone to heaven.

We know not why some lilies wear their
    petals purely white,
Or how they gain their sweet perfume
    we greet with such delight ;
We only know that Jesus made them
    perfect of their kind,
And nature weaves each particle by un-
    seen powers combined :
And so He wrought in that pure life,
    which unto you was given,
Daily to see His precious work in Lizzie,
    gone to heaven.

Ah, well ! the Master knows His own ;
    what need the lily fair
To toil and spin, or spend its strength,
    His great love to declare ;

She only lifts her snowy face, each passer
    by well knows,
It is enough in simple words to say she
    lives and grows :
And so it was this higher work the Lord
    to her had given,
For you could read it in the face of
    Lizzie, gone to heaven.

Ah ! father, mother, on your brows,
    although our eyes are holden,
There surely rests the Spirit's wreath,
    whose flowers and stems are golden ;
Bestowed by Him who giveth back a
    full and plenteous measure,
Because He called you to give up your
    priceless, precious treasure :
And He who drank wrath's bitter cup
    knows how your hearts are riven,
How blank the home, how great the loss
    of Lizzie, gone to heaven.

EDGAR ARCHER.

ONLY twelve summers' suns, twelve
    winters' snows,
Were passed on earth, before those dear
    eyes closed ;
Only twelve years of this small change-
    ful scene,
And now our hearts cry out for that
    which might have been.
We picture him from youth to manhood
    grown,
Many a bright laid scheme from which
    all light hath flown,
Till thought comes back to us with
    weary sigh
And strives to find the clue to that
    mysterious Why.
Full well we know God could have
    spared our boy,
And filled our hearts with thankfulness
    and joy :

He need but speak the Word, death's
    shadow grim
Must yield itself, nor dare contend with
    Him ;
But silence reigned, and the bright spirit
    fled,
Now, now, our sad hearts mourn for
    Edgar dead—
The burden seems too great for us to
    bear,
Our lips are ready with the cry, *Lord*,
    why not spare.

Oh, hush! fond hearts, who can the reason
    tell ?
For He is *God*, and doeth all things well.
Death does not finish thy boy's precious
    life—
Only removes him from this worldly care
    and strife.
Not long had he to fight with Satan's
    power,
Whose darts fall thickest when deep
    sorrows lour ;

Not long had he to kneel and ask for
    grace,
Or plead for clearer growing light from
    Jesus' face;
And now his soul, free from its earthly
    clay,
Oh, how the light of heaven may o'er it
    play!   [Him,
The glowing radiance which comes from
Before whose presence, bright sun, moon,
    and stars are dim.
The bliss of being ever with the Lord,
The depth of rapture which is love's
    reward,   [pain,
Free from all sin, all trial of doubt and
Think, think, cannot your dear one now
    have all this gain?
And time, which makes so many things
    on earth
Become unto our hearts of little worth,
Will but increase the love which God
    hath given,
To link together His redeemed in earth
    and heaven.

And so I think of thee, subdued and sad,
In hallowed sorrow for your little lad,
Over whose grave the sunbeams seem to
　　say—
God's glory yet shall gild the strait and
　　narrow way.

————

TO MRS. ROB,

Whose husband died after a very short illness.

SHORT the summons, brief the message,
　　And yet we must believe it love,
That called him from his earthly duties
　　To the glorious home above.

Scarce time to realise the trial,
　　Strange, mysterious, it must be,
Thy heart still holding hope's last frag-
　　ment,
　　When death's dark shadow compassed
　　thee.

But still, the Lord is ever loving:
  E'en when He takes what most we
    prize,   [darling
There's some good reason why your
  So soon to heavenly life should rise.

So soon leave work and home and loved
    ones,
  The fight, and struggling daily care ;
So soon lay down the earthly weapon,
  And in the higher joy have share.

But thou, sad heart, must mourn and
    sorrow ;
  Not yet canst thou lift up thine eyes
To see the heavenly light, which shineth
  Beyond thy dark, beclouded skies.

And human words sound harsh and
    cruel,
  While human hands are far too rough ;
For thy poor heart so crushed and bleed-
    ing
  We scarce have sympathy enough.

'Tis only He, the Lord of Glory,
  Whose tender touch can soothe and
    heal,   [power,
He killed the *sting* of death's dark
The shadow now is all we feel.

But when the balm of time shall soften
  The bitterness of all thy pain,
Then patience, love, and hope shall
    strengthen,
  Until in heaven you meet again.

———

LITTLE ROBIN.

LITTLE Robin's gone to glory,
  Here his baby lips are mute ;
He has reached the home before thee,
  There to wear his bright new suit.

Suit as white as snow-capped mountain,
  Beautiful beyond compute ;
Washed within the crimson fountain
  Is this glorious new suit.

What it cost, our human powers
   To judge the worth it must refute,
Only within those heavenly bowers
   Can they value that new suit.

Oh, how happy is your darling !
   Sweet his voice as gentle lute ;
Radiant as the sons of morning,
   In that glistening new suit.

Not one tear his bright eye dimming,
   No sound of wrangle or dispute ;
For all his life with joy is brimming,
   As he walks in that new suit.

Free from every sore temptation,
   Which in this world of ill-repute
Tries all our wayward inclinations,
   Until each wears that pure new suit.

Just now when daily care and trial,
   Thy patience tests to unknown bound,
When duties call you by the dozen,
   And life seems but a weary round,

So many things which need attention,
　So many wants to be supplied,
So many pleasures you would give
　　them,
　Which reason says must be denied.

And though your body oft is tired—
　You fain would rest the busy brain,
How sweet to realise the feeling,
　That Robin's life was not in vain!

For while the young ones sing God's
　　praises,
　With voices fresh as morning dew,
The thought of Robin nerves to action,
　And others will be blest through you.

So as the young and tender branches
　Are grafted on the living vine ;
When age comes creeping swiftly on-
　　ward,
　You never, never can repine,

But looking forward to the moment,
   Your lips dear Robin shall salute,
And Jesus gives to you a garment,
   So both shall wear a white new suit.

TO HENRY AND FLORENCE.

You are going to build a home, dear,
   Now mind you do it right;
Making a firm foundation,
   With jewels rare and bright.

Be sure you place the ruby there,
   Rich, warm as glowing love;
Not first unto yourselves, dear,
   But to the Lord above.

Oh, let it shine around your path,
   Your daily portion be;
Remember it was love Divine
   Made Jesus die for thee.

Then let it to each other grow
  More bright and pure each day ;
Making your home the brightest spot
  On all the earthly way.

Then place the emerald's brilliant green
  To shine like faith so true ;
That child-like trust in God's good way,
  As life unfolds to you.

Let not dark doubt its shadow fling
  One moment o'er your mind,
But faith as clear as that green light,
  Your hearts together bind.

Now don't forget the sapphire blue,
  That shines as truth most clear ;
Let God's grand truth, His Holy Word,
  Each day become more dear.

And on this truth an altar build—
  The altar of thy home ;
Where prayers like sweetest incense rise
  From hearts already one.

Let pearls be there for purity,
  In thought, look, word and deed ;
And garnets tell of earnest care,
  For all the daily need.

Hospitality without a grudge
  The amethyst will show ;
And topaz bright, with golden light,
  As earnest friendship glow.

And fix the shaded onyx there,
  For charity most kind ;
Stern self-denial for others' good,
  We oft occasion find.

While round about, and in and out,
  Let turquoise' smiling face,
Keep fresh within your hearts' warm
    home,
  Each loved one's sacred place.

But as the chief grand corner stone,
  Oh, place the diamond there !
For it will tell of blessed work,
  When each may have a share.

M

It will reflect love's glowing hue,
   And faith's clear earnest gaze ;
And every hue that gem can show,
   Is where the diamonds blaze.

So every grace is gathered up,
   In Christ our heavenly King ;
His love will shine upon each need,
   Our daily life can bring.

Then let Him rule within your hearts,
   More perfectly each day ;
Until in His bright blissful home,
   You with Him ever stay.

FRANK'S TROUBLE.

OH, dear ! what a tiresome question to
   me
Is that constant cry of—Frank, what will
   you be ?

My school days are over, and Latin put
    by,   [to try,
No problems to puzzle or French verbs
No theme or analysis is there for me,
But now comes the question—Frank,
    what will you be?

I won't be a lawyer, I don't like the pen,
Nor Bevan, nor Kean, nor my Lord
    Tenterden ;   [suit me,
To stand before big wigs would never
So now comes the question—Frank,
    what will you be?

I won't be a doctor, to cut, blister, bleed,
To send pints of physic where there 's
    little need ;
So much pain and suffering I 've no need
    to see,   [be.
To answer the question of what I will

I won't be a soldier—I never could fight,
As they often do for the wrong, not for
    right ;

To conquer by force could have no
    charm for me,
So still there's that question—Frank,
    what will you be?

I won't be a sailor, a captain or mate,
Unless on our yacht, would no feeling
    elate ;
The storms on the deep I have no wish
    to see,
So now there's that question—Frank,
    what will you be?

There's plenty to choose from, but still
    I'm in doubt,
The thing best to suit me I cannot find
    out ;
And no other person can make choice
    for me,   [be.
And settle the question of what I shall

'Tis no trifle, I tell you, this trouble of
    mine,   [too fine ;
Though some may imagine my fancy's

'Tis business for life, and a great thing
  you see—
A very grave question is what I shall be.

I 'm sure I 've no wish to be wasting my
  time,
But pleasure with work I would like to
  combine ;
As I have the chance it is vexing you
  see,   [be.
Not to settle the question of what I shall

Whatever it is, I 'll be good of the sort,
And work shall be work, then sport will
  be sport ;
When once I am started I 'll press on,
  you see,
Nor disgrace the profession, whate'er it
  may be.

A voice softly whispers, Seek counsel by
  prayer
To Him who has granted each creature
  a share,

To aid in the good and the evil to flee,
He sends us the answer to what we shall
    be.

His wisdom shall make every crooked
    way plain,
And none ever earnestly sought Him in
    vain ;
Then all thy life long 'twill delight thee
    to see   [shall be.
How perfect the answer to what you

TO NELLIE.

JESSAMINE round cottage window,
    Jessamine by leafy bower,
Jessamine on stately terrace,
    Still the same white starry flower.

Growing o'er fantastic rock-work,
    Or some portal old to grace ;
Loved alike by high and lowly
    Is thy bonnie wee white face.

How thy clear cut tiny flowers,
   By thy dark green leaves revealed ;
Though so many budding clusters,
   By the foliage is concealed.

Jessamine, as I gaze upon thee,
   Never shall I make thee vain,
Though gently I may speak thy praises,
   As the thoughts flit through my brain.

Whisper what thy graceful leaflets,
   And thy snowy blossoms teach,
Of those rare and priceless virtues,
   Lying just within our reach.

Thou dost teach of sweet contentment,
   For I 've seen thee green and tall
Spending all thy strength to brighten
   Some dark, sooty London wall.

Thou dost tell of silent working,
   Simply filling well thy place ;
Sending forth thy gentle lessons
   For us mortals to embrace.

Then thy humble obeisances,
    To Summer's faintest breath respond;
Do we show such winning gladness?
    Are we of quick obedience fond?

Do we stand at all times ready
    To answer every one's appeal?
Sympathy in word and action,
    Is it always strong and real?

And when Autumn storms are blowing,
    Though roughly thou be tossed about,
We ne'er can think an angry accent
    Would answer to the wind's wild shout.

So quickly do thy swaying branches
    Return unto their quiet rest?
They make us think of prayer-raised
      fingers
    Pleading for God the soul to bless.

Jessamine, how many lessons
    Could thou teach, if I would learn,
Were my spirit higher, purer,
    All thy beauties to discern!

Other minds may read the clearer,
　　Other pens thy virtues tell,
Other lips may sing thy praises,
　　But, Jessamine, I love thee well.

TO MAY.

OH, tell me, do you love them, our bonnie
　　English lanes,
With the freshness of their verdure where
　　a wealth of beauty reigns?
Oh, have you sauntered through them on
　　a balmy day in June,
When buds were opening sweetly, and
　　all nature seemed in tune;
And marked the glowing colours which
　　bank and hedge adorn,
Blending there like a gay mosaic, in
　　quaintly varied form?
And in what wondrous beauty each
　　separate blossom grows,
What multitudes of tints and shade
　　leaflet and petal shows!

Look at yon climbing bindweed, with
    cups so purely white,
And lingering tufts on hawthorn
    boughs to give us keen delight ;
But of all the wayside beauties there's
    none so sweetly fair,
As our bonnie English wild-rose which
    shows its flowerets there.
No gardener attends it, no toil or care it
    needs,
But it springs forth in its beauty from
    among the lowly weeds.
We welcome in the spring time its sprays
    of brown or green,
And through all the summer brightness
    what a wealth of blossom's seen ;
Even the cold of winter its brightness
    will not slay,
Can you count the glowing berries hang-
    ing on every spray?
And May is like the wild-rose, sweet,
    winsome, bright, and true,
Standing forth firm and steadfast, with
    warmth of love for you.

When once rose-buds are open, and the
    bee can creep within,
It is sure to find some nectar to carry
    'neath its wing ;
And from the yellow centre it gathers
    many a store
Of sweet and luscious honey, valued by
    rich and poor.
So if we ope the portal of our May's
    loving heart,
We shall find the golden centre and
    ne'er from it depart ;
And if she shows some prickles—for a
    rose will have a thorn—
She will not mean to hurt us or really
    make us mourn.
So as we gather roses from the hedge in
    sunny June,
And gaze upon its beauty and sing its
    praise in tune ;
So we will fondly cherish, while heart's
    warm pulses beat,
Our May's a precious treasure which
    makes our lives more sweet.

TO MRS. K.

How can I tread this thorny path,
  Dark, rugged, bleak, and wild?
I shrink, as from some winter blast
  Retreats the timid child.

Those flinty stones, those briery thorns,
  My feeble steps delay;
Is there no *smoother* path for me
  To tread the narrow way?

This heavy weight of constant care
  To which each day gives birth,
Like iron bands, hard, firm, and strong,
  They press me down to earth.

My children have such varied needs,
  They many things dislike;
How shall I help each untried heart
  To seek the Lord aright?

Oh, teach me, Lord, the way to live,
   Aright my cross to bear ;
For Thou didst shed Thy precious blood
   That I Thy joy should share.

But what is this, for as I gaze
   A change comes o'er the scene ;
No longer dark, for glowing light
   Shines with a mellow beam.

Those flinty stones look straight and
     smooth,
   And with the thorns are flowers,
While angel hands now beckon me
   Unto their leafy bowers ;

And underneath this weight of care
   I see two nail-pierced hands ;
Which bear the load, till scarce I feel
   The pressure of its bands.

Still as I gaze, my children dear
   Before me seem to pass ;
Methinks I see their future clear,
   As mirrored in a glass.

First Lizzie, gentle, patient grown,
  How sweet her rule of love ;
Those pierced hands are leading on
  With unseen power above.

Then Dora, mild, obedient child,
  Goes on her quiet way ;
She hears the Saviour's loving voice,
  And serves Him day by day.

Next Hilda, active, bright, and quick,
  What ready help she gives,
With self-denial, for the sake
  Of Christ, in whom she lives.

Now follows Mabel, sweet young flower,
  She too will seek His face ;
And, drinking from the well of life,
  Go on from grace to grace.

Tibby and Baby, though so young,
  For them God's love is free,
As when He called the little ones
  And said, Come unto Me.

And now the vision fades away,
  While tears bedew my cheek ;
I, in the quiet darkness, lay
  Close to the Saviour's feet.

Lord, wilt Thou do all this, I cry,
  If so, my path is clear ;
I 'll take my cross up day by day
  Without a doubt or fear.

Thy Word to teach, Thy love to guide,
  Thy Sabbaths duly given ;
And Jesus ever at my side,
  Through life in death to heaven.

THOUGHTS ON THE 31ST OF MAY.

TWELVE months more of time is past,
Another year has o'er us cast
      Its many shades and lights ;
For hope is still our guiding star,
Though oft it glimmers faintly far,
      And nearly out of sight.

Little change this year hath seen,
And slight improvement has there been
 'Twixt this year and the last;
And prayer must make faith's anchor
 sure,
Or else it never can endure
 And keep her moorings fast.
Yes! prayer to Him who yet can give
Us patience 'midst our trial to live,
 Nor murmur at His will;
And taking up our cross each day,
Press on with joy the narrow way
 O'ercoming every ill.
But oh! these sinful hearts of ours,
How slight their faith, how weak their
 powers
 To hold the promise fast;
We want ourselves to work and do,
And cannot see that glorious view
 When all the struggle's past.
The view when on that dreadful day,
That He, the Truth, the Life, the
 Way,
 Was lifted up for sin;

And bore the fearful untold load,
That awful weight, the wrath of God,
  Eternal peace to win.
Oh, could we know the mighty love
He felt, when from His home above
  He came our work to do,
With joy we'd bear each trial and pain,
And count each loss but blissful gain
  With Him so clear in view.
Oh, may His heavenly grace be shed
In rich abundance o'er thy head,
  May peace dwell in thine heart ;
The precious pearl of love be thine,
Through all thy life its lustre shine,
  Quenching each fiery dart ;
And if no more mine eyes shall see
The varied tints in sky or tree,
  Of Nature's glorious dress ;
No more my foot shall press the sod
When spread abroad the works of God
  In all their loveliness ;
No more, as in the western sky
The sun in all its majesty
  Sets in a flood of gold,

N

Making each fence, tree-stump and stone
Glow with a beauty not its own,
      I may no more behold ;
If all the rest of my life's day
I 'm doomed on this sick couch to lay
      And strength no more shall come,
May grace be sent us from above,
That we can feel God still is love,
      And say, Thy will be done.

TO MY HUSBAND.

FAIN would I write some loving words,
    To make your heart beat high ;
Fain would I catch some noble thought
    And fix it ere it fly.

Fain would I pen some words of fire
    With glowing pathos rife,
To strengthen every good desire,
    And brighten all thy life.

But, like a bird on drooping wing,
  I cannot soar on high ;
Down, down to earth my spirits cling,
  My eloquence a sigh.

My words are languid, poor and weak,
  No life within them glow ;
They 'll ne'er revive the power I seek,
  So meaningless they flow.

Oh, for a dash of brilliant thought,
  That I might give to thee
Some strain more worthy of the day
  Of thy nativity.

When I would gather from all good,
  To lay it at thy feet,
Nor deem the offering fair enough,
  Thy joyful smile to meet ;

But earthly gifts too worthless seem,
  The heart's wish to express ;
Their tinsel value light I deem
  A trouble to redress.

Then I will ask for higher bliss
Than this world can bestow,
May faith, joy, peace and happiness
Increase while here below.

And may the Holy Comforter
Within thy heart now dwell,
And Jesus Christ reveal Himself
As thine Emmanuel.

———

MAGGIE'S HANDS.

LITTLE fingers, oh! how busy, washing,
work_ing, day by day,
Ever o'er some object flitting, making
work seem more like play.
Little fingers, oh! how lightly they can
touch the aching brow,
Passing o'er the work so slightly, how
they move before me now.

Little fingers, oft I watch thee, as some
    hidden mystery,
Wondering what may be the future
    weaving of thy destiny ;
Thou dost speak to me in language now
    half-hidden, half-revealed,
Showing many little glimpses which to
    others are concealed.
Thou dost tell of timid shyness, many a
    needless fear misplaced,
And a want of self-reliance brings the
    hot blood to thy face ;
Thou dost tell of quick emotion, and the
    hasty spoken word
Which has scarcely passed lips' portal,
    than you wish it was not heard :
Thou dost tell of clinging purpose, hard
    to alter, change, or move—
I don't mind, 'tis just what *I* think, what
    you say does nothing prove—
Thou dost tell of indignation if a thing
    but seem unjust,
You at once would have it altered before
    you think which way is best ;

And there's yet another feeling, which
    oft a stumbling-block may be,
Only think, one cannot help it, 'tis
    reason quite enough for thee ;
Thou dost tell of strong affections, deep
    and constant though not shown,
In a time of grief and trouble, then thy
    worth would best be known.
Fingers, I must leave off writing ; are my
    words both clear and true ?
Then I think that sister Maggie knows
    just what I think of you.

TO OUR SISTER IN IRELAND.

MAY happiness and peace be thine,
And that bright joy which is Divine
    Dwell in thy heart ;
So as each year shall roll away
May grace be thine from day to day
    To do thy part.

All that sweet power He can give,
Within thy being richly live
    And work aright;
So shall each piece of labour be
A blessed, true reality,
    Done with all might.
May each creation of thy brain
Help to encourage and sustain
    Some noble thought;
That as the sands of time depart,
In this life's work you leave thy mark
    So clearly wrought,
That others by thy work shall learn
To hate all evil, and to spurn
    Things low and base;
Then onward, upward they will press,
Each for a crown of righteousness,
    Through God's great grace.

———

DEAR JENNIE.

LYING on a bed of sickness,
  Full of weakness, suffering, pain,
This thought comes hovering o'er me—
  Shall I ever rise again?

Will the pleasant April breezes
  Ever fan my wasted cheek?
Or with cheerful hearty accent
  Shall I friend and neighbour greet?

All around are many loved ones—
  Father kind, and sisters dear;
And my tender, loving mother,
  At my bedside ever near.

Now my John sits quiet by me,
  With earnest gaze and loving heart,
And an infant form of beauty
  Seems to cry, we cannot part.

And on this Sabbath afternoon
   When the Big-Kirk bell has ceased,
Plants, flowers, and all around me
   Breathe an atmosphere of peace.

While I think of other loved ones
   Who have homes so far away,
When the evening shadows gather,
   Will for me so humbly pray,

That I may have strength now given
   To take up my cross aright,
And truly do or suffer,
   As most needful in God's sight ;

In love, should He my health restore,
   May I rightly live each day ;
In my thoughts and words and actions
   Pressing on the narrow way.

Should He see fit to call me hence,
   To that glorious home above,
Then I ever shall be praising
   His great and wondrous love.

When a few more years have passèd,
  May I meet each loving one,
Therefore my grateful lips shall cry,
  Father ! Thy will be done.

———

TO WEE FORRY.

Far away in Bonnie Scotland,
  Fanned by the healthful breeze,
There stands a pleasant cottage,
  Shaded by waving trees.

And in that cottage lives a lad—
  A good one I am sure ;
Now do you wish to know his name—
  They call him Forry Muir.

But Forry has been very sick,
  So weak, so low, and sad ;
And truly sorry still I feel
  For this same little lad.

He could not walk, he could not play,
   Nor could he lie quite still ;
But tossed about from side to side,
   He was so very ill.

His grandmother with anxious care
   To every want attends ;
And many an earnest heartfelt prayer
   For him to Heaven ascends.

Now courage take, thou loving heart !
   Thy prayer is heard above ;
Health and strength once more shall
     come
   Unto the child you love.

And so it was, for bright and clear
   Those childish eyes now shone ;
Oh ! cast away each gloomy fear,
   The fever's power is gone.

And here I fain would end my rhyme,
   But trouble is not past,
For once again is Forry Muir
   On bed of sickness cast.

Look, look, the sight is sad to see—
  Here comes at rapid rate,
A horse has taken sudden fright,
  He nears the churchyard gate.

Quick! save the child, oh, save the
    child,
  He still is very weak!
Ah, 'tis too late, for there he lay,
  And cannot move or speak.

And once again dear grandmother
  The loving nurse must be;
For pain is very hard to bear,
  And makes us sad to see.

But Forry will be very good,
  In patience bear the pain;
And then I hope we soon shall hear
  He's getting well again.

So now good-bye, if you like this
  I think you may be sure
That Aunt will try to write again
  To little Forry Muir.

OUR BOYS.

Our boys! what would we have them—
   Why earnest, brave, and true,
Seeking each day something to learn,
   And noble act to do.

With bright and cheerful spirits,
   No shade upon their brow,
Thorough in study, play, and work,
   We want them happy now.

Oh, boys, what wondrous power
   Dwells in your mind and heart!
To help in all this busy life
   Where each should do his part.

For you *must* help or hinder
   The progress of the right,
And every action, look, and word,
   Will go to swell its might.

We want you strong, yet gentle,
　With courage to say No ;
Not daunted by a sneer or laugh
　Wherever you may go.

Oh, take the higher view of life,
　And close your doings scan ;
Remember, every boy who lives
　Is father to the man.

———

OUR CHAPEL.

LET me say a few words, with a hearty
　good will,
Of a place near to London, 'tis called
　Buckhurst Hill ;
Not a detailed account of houses or
　people,
The age, style of the church, and the
　height of the steeple,

But there's one little spot you might
pass any day,
'Tis so modest a building you'd ne'er
glance that way—
To describe it aright might an architect
baffle,
But folks about here call it Wesleyan
Chapel.

Though the outside is grim—there is
nought to admire—
Yet within, we believe, oft are sparks of
true fire;
Though 'tis rather the work than the
building, I guess,
That lays claim to the thought which
I wish to express.

Meditate on the power of heart, mind,
and brain,
Which the members united within them
contain,

With a super like Ingram, whose spirit
    so mild
Makes us think of the Master when
    blessing a child.

When sermons breathe forth from
    hearts full of love,
And descend on the hearers like a
    peace-giving dove,
And prayers are heart breathings of
    fervent desires,   [aspires.
Towards holier living each member

When the singing is true from the lip
    and the heart,
Real thanksgiving to God that in Christ
    we have part ;
When classes are met for improving
    each other,   [brother ;
With true family greeting of sister and

Where the prayer-meetings all are com-
    munions with God,
And we follow the steps which the
    Master has trod,

With a schoolroom quite full, as each
    Sabbath comes round,
Super, teachers, and scholars in love's
    work may abound.

Thus in union complete, with the Spirit
    to guide,
What a wondrous power in this spot
    might abide !
For as trickling rill from a green moun-
    tain side,   [its tide,
Till it reaches the ocean and flows with

So the spirit that's pure, by the might
    of the Lord,
In each pathway of life will abide by
    His Word,   [bless,
To comfort or strengthen, encourage and
Any brother or sister in want or distress.

And implore them to seek for the com-
    fort Divine,
Until infinite love through their daily
    life shine,

So we still prize the building where there's nought to admire—
No melodious organ to lead on the choir;
It boasts not of Gothic or Saxon or Grecian,
The glass is all plain, not rich tinted Venetian ;

No Corinthian columns our fine taste to please,
And the seats seem invented our comfort to tease,
But if God's Spirit's here, though we've no cushioned stall,
Our Wesleyan Chapel's right dear to us all.

———

HOUSEKEEPING DIFFICULTIES WITH TWO YOUNG SERVANTS.

Now, Emily, why will you do the thing
    that is not right,
I cannot trust the least to you, when
    working out of sight :
Oh, Lizzie, see how black you are, what
    are you doing, child,
The soot upon your hands and face's
    enough to make one wild.
Just look at those potatoes, girl, they
    are not half done through,
And cabbage leaf is near as stiff as when
    on stalk it grew.
Mind, Emily, your master's boots clean
    ere you go upstairs,
I will not have them standing there
    until there are two pairs.
I strongly do object to have the dusting
    done in stripes,
'Tis rubbing keeps the polish on, and
    not those gentle wipes :

Now, do you think the whiting should
    be left upon each spoon?
You are finishing at six o'clock what
    should be done by noon.
There, Lizzie, see those knives are left,
    though dinner is at two,
Oh, girl, I wish you would give heed to
    what I say to you ;
Good gracious, see those dish covers, no
    sweep could make them blacker,
Well, dirt, I think, agrees with you, for
    really you are fatter.

So I go on from day to day, like ever-
    sounding bell,
With just this difference in our tongues
    that tolls *I* have to tell ;
And yet there must some reason be for
    all this daily fuss,   [worry thus ;
It never is my wish, I know, the girls should
Oh, patience, come, my old tried friend,
    help me jog on apace,
To reach the peace which always comes
    to those who run The race.

ON RECEIVING HALF-A-SOVER-EIGN FOR MY DORCAS FROM AN UNKNOWN FRIEND.

OH, thou little bit of gold,
Can thy worth by me be told?
Looking on thee I can see
Many things to do with thee.
Calico and flannel too,
Outer garments not a few ;
When the winter comes again,
And the little ones complain,
Thy help will make them warm and snug,
With a blanket, frock, or rug,
Covering many a shivering limb,
Thou wee, brilliant, golden thing.
Showing how true love did grow
In the heart that could bestow
Thee on me to use for others,
Sad and suffering sisters, brothers.
Trusting me, that I may do
The very best I can with you,
May the one who sent thee here,
Find the Master very near ;

Know His love and see His smile
Beaming on her all the while ;
Giving back in fullest measure
Of her heart's most precious treasure ;
Filling up unto the brim
Every day with joy in Him.
So each year will gather up
God's own gold into Life's cup.

Now, on behalf of many poor,
Deep, warm thanks from Emma Muir.

DOCTOR LLYLE.

WHEN people now are very ill,
Away with plaster, draught, or pill,
What need to treat them in that style—
Copy the clever Dr. Llyle.
No embrocation doth he need
To bring back health with mighty speed
But doctors with a word and smile,
So works the wonderful Dr. Llyle.

No journey long doth he them send,
Protesting it their health will mend ;
No patient would he thus beguile,
Far simpler works great Dr. Llyle.
No shock of battery need you bear
To get your health in good repair,
I never heard it all the while,
One shock was given by Dr. Llyle.
No seaside lodging must you take,
Where money melts like small snow-flake,
Such wasteful ways he would revile—
Far cuter man is Dr. Llyle.
And as for German mud-baths too,
Be sure he'll not send me or you,
But, holding such as fashion's wile,
That's not my cure, says Dr. Llyle.
And, one thing more than all of these,
I never heard him ask for fees,
So even if you had the bile
You'd not get cross with Dr. Llyle.
Now let us wish him all good speed,
For health and happiness we need,
And in return at him we'll smile,
And bid good-day to Dr. Llyle.

CURLING; OR, BEEF AND GREENS.

YOU bid me in verse
My thought now rehearse,
   But how shall I manage a line,
With you far away,
This slow passing day,
   And such hard throbbing pain all the
     time?

'Tis no love to roam
That takes you from home,
   And your health 's worth the tenderest
     care;
Yet fain there I 'd be,
The loved faces to see,
   And the warm earnest welcome to
     share.

I can fancy the scene
The frost must have been,
   With the sunlight on each tiny spray;

Making great your delight
To witness the sight,
    As the train bore you swiftly away.

My thoughts swiftly turn
To mountain and burn,
    Or the loch where the curlers are met ;
Those big curling stone—
Each plays with his own,
    And some think theirs the very best
    set.

Hark to the glad shout
From all round about—
    Well done (Beef and Greens)! Forry
    Muir !
The sound lingers long,
As loath to be gone,
    Then floats faintly away o'er the
    moor.

Among all the rest,
And doing his best,
    Though seldom he's seen on the spot,

Is young Forry Muir,
And you may be sure,
   He will give them a very fair shot.

The game still goes on,
The victory's won ;
   When the sun's sinking low in the
     west,
Each object looks gay
In its bright glowing ray,
   And the curlers are needing a rest.

The bright stars above
Seem to look down in love
   From the sky where they twinkling
     shine ;
As if they would say,
Walk the strait narrow way,
   Live each day in the love that's
     Divine.

If ever I come
To my Scottish home,
   When winter has ice bound each brook,

'Twill my journey repay
If I can, any day,
  At the curlers just have a good look.

My thoughts I call back,
From the curlers' bright track,
  Though my sympathy still with them
    leans ;
So a happy new year
Unto each curler here,
  May you all often get " Beef and
    Greens."

MARGATE.

On the jetty, on the jetty,
  Where the girls delight to flirt—
To show how small their waists are,
  And how short or long their skirt.

Should the feet be small and pretty,
  And the ankle well turned too,

You may be sure the skirt is short,
Perhaps high heeled the shoe.

Should the foot be large and ugly,
And not well shaped one bit,
Oh, be quite sure the robe is long,
Though so nicely it may fit.

Here are many kinds of chignons,
Large and small and round and
square;
They do not always suit the face,
Though they show off so much hair.

On the jetty, on the jetty,
Where the band plays every day;
But, remember, if you listen
You will also have to pay.

I think pay must be the watch-word
Of the folks now living here;
No matter what it is you want,
They will make you pay so dear.

Should you be strolling on the sands
  For a quiet evening walk,
And you wander on unthinking,
  Engaged in earnest talk ;

When suddenly you are brought to—
  There runs just across your path
The water, which is deep enough
  To give both your feet a bath.

You stop to think what's best to do,
  Over it you cannot spring,
But there are large stones near to you
  Which are just the very thing.

Over you go, but scarce have placed
  On the dryer sand your feet,
When standing there, awaiting you,
  A boy or man you meet.

With touch of cap, and, If you please,
  Now a copper, sir, for me,
For putting of them stones down there
  To keep you from the sea.

And thus it is where'er you go,
  To the jetty, pier, or sand,
Along the town to the parade—
  There's always some demand.

On, on it goes from day to day,
  Till patience, pocket, purse
Is near worn out ; but really I
  Must finish now this verse.

So, friend, your kind indulgence grant
  To all the faults here penned—
I scarcely think they will reward
  Your reading to the end.

———

LORIMER AND GILLIES, PRINTERS, EDINBURGH.

www.ingramcontent.com/pod-product-compliance
Lightning Source LLC
Chambersburg PA
CBHW030130030726
47498CB00007B/2630